Rise of the Dominants

Master's

FATE

Red Phoenix

Copyright © 2019 Red Phoenix
Print Edition
www.redphoenixauthor.com

Master's Fate: Rise of the Dominants
Second Book of the Trilogy

Cover by Shanoff Designs
Formatted by BB eBooks
Phoenix symbol by Nicole Delfs

Dedication

How I loved writing about Master Anderson!

I hope, dear readers, you sigh with desire, shed some tears, and snort-laugh like I did while reading the story.

I have to thank MrRed for all the inspiration and support. I will never forget the night we celebrated "The End". You made it so special.

I must also thank my editor, Kh Koehler, who walks by my side through the craziness, making sure I meet my deadline. Big hugs, my friend!

I want to give a shout out to my betas. Kathy, who shares what she's learned and helped me to liven up an important scene. Becki, who catches those mistakes nobody else sees. Marilyn, who remembers everything about the series–I love that!

Big thanks to Brenda, a dedicated fan who continues to help me keep up with the craziness behind the scenes. A Master Anderson fan, I loved reading her reactions when she got this story.

To Anthony, my literary advisor, he'll never know how thankful I am for the changes he's brought to my life and career.

I can't forget my marketing team! Jon and Jessica, your enthusiasm and hard work has made such a difference. How lucky am I to get to work with you every day!

I have deep love for my muses. Time and time again, they carry me along with the stories they have to tell. They've never let me down, and I will forever be grateful to them.

And last, but not least, a huge thankyou to my fans. I love spending time with you through my stories, interacting online, and at my book signings. I seriously just want to hug you all!

SIGN UP FOR MY NEWSLETTER HERE FOR THE LATEST RED PHOENIX UPDATES

SALES, GIVEAWAYS, NEW RELEASES, PREORDER LINKS, AND MORE!

SIGN UP HERE

REDPHOENIXAUTHOR.COM/NEWSLETTER-SIGNUP

Get the rest of the trilogy now!

Sir's Rise, Book 1

The Russian Reborn, Book 3

CONTENTS

glee

(note from the author)

In the D/s dynamic, the Dominant's title is capitalized and the submissive's pet name is not.

It speaks to the power exchange between them and is a meaningful representation of the relationship in written form.

Summer Kink

I slap my roommate on the back feeling a sense of loss knowing I won't be seeing him again until the fall semester begins. "Going to miss you, buddy."

"Same here," Thane answers. "I have to admit, it's going to be odd not waking up in the middle of the night to you talking in your sleep."

I snort in protest. "I don't talk in my sleep."

"Yes, you do."

"Why are you just telling me now?"

"I didn't want you to lose sleep over it."

I chuckle. Thane has a subtle sense of humor. I'm glad to see him using it—it makes me proud that I've had that kind of influence over him, because the guy was *way* too serious when we first met.

"So, tell me. What do I talk about?"

Thane only answers with a smirk.

I nudge him in the ribs. "I deserve to know don't you think?"

"Let's just say I know where your...*unique* passions

lie."

"Oh, shit," I mutter, sweeping my hair back. I wonder what the hell came out of my mouth while I was dreaming.

"Don't worry. Your secret's safe with me."

His serious expression leads me to think it's much worse than I imagine, and I laugh nervously. "Now you've got me worried. God only knows the crazy things my subconscious comes up with when I'm sleeping."

"It's demented," Thane agrees.

I snort in amusement, trusting he's just having a little fun with me. "Okay, out with it. What the hell do I say?"

He shakes his head slowly, a sympathetic look on his face.

"Look, I'll wrestle it out of you if I have to."

Thane states with confidence, "I'll take you down if you try."

My low laughter fills the dorm room. "Are you really trying to start something with me?"

He raises an eyebrow in challenge.

"I'm certain you're only goading me on, but that would be foolish of you since I am the *master* of pranks. You'd be giving me a whole summer to plan my revenge."

Feeling generous, I tell him, "Because you have no idea what you're starting here, I'll let you back out now—no harm, no foul. Just tell me what I say in my sleep."

Instead of backing down, he answers, "What you murmur in your sleep is so perverted, it would keep your poor mother up at night."

By mentioning my mama, Thane's crossed a line. There's *no* way I'm letting him back out now. "You really want to rumble, do ya?"

"Bring on your worst," he challenges with a smirk.

"You *do* realize you're playing with fire."

He nods. "I happen to like it hot."

I chuckle to myself, accepting Thane's challenge. I'm going to get him so good that even though he knows it's coming at some point and time, the poor bastard still won't see it coming.

I rub my hands together, relishing the thought.

This is going to be my best damn prank yet…

I feel a flood of exhilaration as I stare out the airplane window when my plane finally lands in Denver. I've failed to realize how much I've missed the Rockies until I see them again, standing majestically in the distance.

While the ocean may be awe-inspiring, nothing beats those ragged peaks covered in snow…

To my surprise, not only does my family meet me at the airport, but also a bunch of my buddies from high school.

It does a fella's heart good to have my posse around me.

"Brad, Brad, Brad!" a small group of my old girl-friends chant. I'm a lucky guy, because every girl I've ever dated still remains a good friend of mine.

To be completely frank, I *love* women. I don't care

what they look like, their level of popularity, body-type or race. I love the fairer sex and treat them all with the respect they deserve—I always have.

The fact that I know how to treat a lady is due to my parents, who instilled that in me at an early age. You see, my parents are the gold standard I hold all my relationships to. The day I find the woman who completes my world, I will happily settle down.

Until then…

I plan to enjoy every woman who wants to dance in the sheets with me. In my humble opinion, women are far too lovely to ignore.

I walk toward my welcome party with arms outstretched, giving my mama a hug first. She's tiny compared to me, so I have to bend down to hug her. She looks up at me with those twinkling green eyes and smiles tenderly.

"I've missed you, Ma."

"Missed you, too," she says, her eyes tearing up as she gives me an extra tight squeeze before letting go.

I look over at my sisters and the rest of my family and friends gathered here, and I'm hit with how much their support means to me. I feel a tinge of sorrow for my friend Thane. It makes me more determined than ever to bring him home with me for Christmas this year.

Oh, shit…

It just came to me what my prank will be. Score!

Hot damn. Thane is totally in for it now.

After greeting my family, I give Sofia, the girl with the beautiful, long brown hair and mischievous glint in her eye, an extra-long hug. I whisper in her ear with a seductive growl, "I have something to show you in the barn tonight."

After I break the embrace, she looks up at me, a grin spreading across her face as she discretely glances down at my crotch. "I can't wait to see it."

Little does she know I have chosen her to be the first to experience my bullwhip. Her adventurous spirit and total frankness ensure that she will be open and honest during our session together. Not all women are assertive enough to be completely honest with themselves about what they want, but Sofia is a woman bursting with confidence.

I head home with my posse in tow and they spoil me with an old-fashioned country gathering. My parents have planned a huge celebration for me, complete with a long picnic table covered in Ma's down-home cooking.

My welcome home party includes plenty of tall tales shared by my elders, good eats, and the lively sound of my uncle's fiddle, which causes impromptu line dancing as we finish the evening's festivities.

Damn, I've missed this life.

Sofia waits patiently as all the other guests leave. I've had a difficult time keeping my cock in check, knowing I'm about to introduce her to my whip. There is a sensual thrill in being the first to expose her to something kinky—something she has never even considered.

Of course, there is always the risk she will say no, but that only makes it more exhilarating for me.

I love a good challenge.

Once all the other guests have gone, I casually wrap my arms around Sofia's waist as I tell my family, "I gotta tell ya, I've been missing home something fierce."

My father smiles knowingly. "I'm certain everyone has been missing you, including Rebel. Why don't you take Sofia down to the barn to see her? I've got a new mare for you to check out, as well. With our herd growing, we've been in need of extra horsepower."

I appreciate not only my father's pun, but that he's making it easy for me to spend some much-needed alone time with Sofia. "Glad to hear things are going well with the ranch, Pop."

"We've seen a slow but steady increase in sales after pledging to raise our animals in an organic environment. Since it aligns with my own philosophy about raising healthy livestock, it only made sense to make the commitment. But, as you know, it has been a tough road."

I slap him on the back. "I'm proud of you for sticking it out. Every animal deserves to be treated with care and respect."

Pop smiles at me before giving Sofia a wink. He leads my mama into the house, offering to help her with the dishes.

I take Sofia's hand and head toward the horse barn in the lower pasture. It's situated far enough away from the ranch house that it will give us the privacy we need to enjoy ourselves. As we walk hand in hand, I mention with a grin, "You probably think you know what I want to show you."

She stares at my growing hard-on stretching the material of my jeans and her lips curve into a smile. "You've made it quite obvious, Brad."

I stop for a moment, looking deep into her eyes. "I

want to try something new. Something that's kind of kinky."

"Ooh…I like the sound of that." She squeezes my hand confidently, her eyes flashing with excitement.

As soon as I open the barn door, the horses greet us with low nickers. I head straight to my mare. She starts prancing excitedly in place as I approach. "Miss me, girl?"

She lowers her head so I can pet her, nickering with pleasure as I caress her face with both hands.

"Yeah, I've missed you, too."

Sofia stands back, observing our reunion and laughs softly. "I'm not sure whether to feel jealous or not."

I chuckle, kissing the soft area above Rebel's upper lip. "No need to feel jealous. I was six when I had the privilege of seeing this filly born. Pop spoiled me that night by giving her to me."

"Wow, that must be the longest relationship you've ever had with a girl," Sofia teases. "No wonder I'm jealous."

I laugh. Grabbing Sofia around the waist, I pull her to me. "Want to know a secret?"

She glances up at me, grinning. "Sure."

"Her name isn't really Rebel. Pop gave her that name because he insisted that she sound like a respectable working horse."

"What's her real name?"

"Hot Chocolate," I answer with a wink.

Sofia looks at my mare and coos. "That's so darn cute."

I pet Hot Chocolate's nose again as I explain, "That

night in the barn, I told my pop that she was the color of hot chocolate and that's what I wanted to name her."

"And he said no?"

"Yep. The ranch hands would have given me all kinds of grief if I called her that, so I totally understand Pop's reasoning on the name change. However, I have a stubborn streak a mile long and always call her Hot Chocolate in private." I press my cheek against the mare's cheek, rubbing behind her ears just the way she likes it. "It's been our little secret even since, hasn't it, girl?"

She nickers again, turning her head so I can reach both ears.

The horse in the next stall starts pawing the ground and huffing, wanting attention. I glance over and see Pop has purchased a roan mare. I look back at Hot Chocolate and chuckle. "Got yourself a new roomie, huh? Let me guess. She's a bit too serious…"

I laugh, giving Hot Chocolate one more rub before I give the new horse a pat on the nose. Then, I turn my full attention on Sofia.

"So, what exactly is your kinky proposal?" she asks lustfully, sidling up next to me.

"Before I say another word, I *must* kiss those luscious lips." I push her against the barn wall, pressing my growing erection against her. "I have waited too long to taste this succulent mouth…"

As I slowly lean down to give her a passionate kiss, I suddenly hear a bunch of girlish kissing noises behind me.

Damn, I've just been cockblocked.

I turn to see my three sisters standing there with smirks on their faces. I shake my head slowly.

Sisters.

When Sofia sees them, however, she totally freezes. Looking up at me, she asks in the barest of whispers, "You want me to do it with…them?"

I burst out laughing. "Oh, hell no!"

I glance back at the giggling trio, stating as I shoo them toward the door, "You are about to leave, aren't you, girls?"

"But, Brad, we just wanted to watch you make kissy face with Sofia," Christina teases.

"Not happening," I tell her as I gently shove my youngest sister out the barn door.

"You spoil all our fun…" Ruthie complains as I guide her out, too.

I glance at Megan, the oldest of the three. She happens to be sporting a wicked grin. I suspect she's the one who put the other two up to this.

"Don't do anything I wouldn't do, big brother…" she tells me as she leaves.

I shut the barn doors behind her, then turn back to Sofia, concerned that their intrusion has just ruined our evening adventures.

"I don't suppose you're still in the mood?"

She wraps her arms around my waist. "I'm always in the mood for your kisses."

"Oh, I like that answer…" I growl as I kiss her, letting loose the passion that has been building the entire evening.

She purrs when I pull away. "Damn it, Brad. I forgot

just how weak your kisses make me. I'm afraid I'd say yes to almost anything—even your sisters."

My low chuckle fills the barn as I brush my finger against her lower lip. "What I have planned is just between you and me." I kiss her again, groaning when she opens her lips and my tongue enters her mouth.

God, I could take her right now. But I've been waiting too long to introduce her to my whip, so I command my cock to be patient.

As if reading my mind, Sofia asks with a seductive smile, "So, cowboy, what kinky thing do you want to show me?"

Whip Me

I pull a red bandana from my pocket and roll it up diagonally to use as a blindfold. Placing it over her eyes, I tie a knot to secure it and tell her, "Wait here while I get it for you."

I feel her tremble and hear the excitement in her voice when she asks, "Get what, exactly?"

Sofia has no idea where I'm taking her tonight…

I choose not to answer, giving her a parting kiss before I open the barn door to leave. "Don't move," I command on my way out.

My experience at the dungeon has taught me that making a woman wait makes an interesting form of foreplay.

I smile to myself as I walk to Pop's truck and pull my duffle bag out from the back. As I head back to the barn, I make a quick check of the perimeter to verify my sisters aren't planning another sneak attack.

Convinced we're alone, I reenter the barn and shut the door, wedging a rake between the two handles so no one can disturb us again.

Sofia turns her head toward me, laughing nervously. "I was starting to worry you were playing a practical joke on me, Brad."

I wrap my arm around her. "I would never be cruel to you, Sofia. Unless, of course, you wanted me to be…"

I feel her shiver in my arms and my heart starts to race. I'm unsure how she will react to my unusual proposal. There's a thrill to it—an unexpected high that comes from exposing my kink to someone unfamiliar with BDSM.

"Hold out your hands, Sofia."

I place my coiled-up bullwhip in her open palms. It has some heft to it, and she gasps in surprise.

"Do you know what it is?"

"I can tell it's made of leather because of the smell…and I love leather."

"I do, too," I reply lustfully. Loosening the tie of the blindfold, I let it fall away. Sofia looks down at my favorite whip and says nothing, but I watch as goose-bumps rise on her skin.

"I…" she stammers. "I don't understand."

I slowly trail a finger down her arm, taking hold of the whip she holds. "I want to use my bullwhip on you."

She shudders, her eyes growing wide as she stares at the instrument.

"I am very skilled with the whip," I assure her, nibbling lightly on her neck.

"Is this what people do in LA?" she murmurs, closing her eyes as she gives into my sexual advances.

"It is," I answer, biting her neck with more intensity.

"Oh, Brad…"

I put my finger to her lips and say in a low, gravelly tone, "Tonight, you will call me Master."

I feel her stiffen in my arms and her eyes pop open. "Master? I don't think so."

I know she has a strong spirit, which is why I chose her for my first. So I continue with my seduction, willingly risking her rejection.

"This is my kink, Sofia. Do you think you're woman enough to handle it?"

She stares into my eyes and then glances down at the whip. "It scares me."

I unfurl it so she can see its full length. "I will only take you as far as you're willing to go. I promise it will be like nothing you have ever experienced before."

For emphasis, I snap my whip and the crack of it echoes in the air, causing her to jump.

Sofia shakes her head. "No, this is too much—I can't."

My heart constricts, knowing she's turning me down, but I hide my disappointment from her. Coiling the bullwhip back up, I realize I've come on too strong. Being used to the subs at the dungeon, I've lost perspective on how strange my offer would seem in the vanilla world.

Still…I'm convinced she would enjoy it.

Lifting her chin, I kiss her on the lips and say confidently, "When you're ready, Sofia, I'll be waiting to show you a whole new world of pleasure."

I put my whip back in the duffle bag and smile at her, wanting her to know it's cool between us. Taking her hand, I start walking her out.

"Brad…" she says haltingly.

"Yes?"

"Maybe I do want to take a little peek into that world with you."

"Tonight?"

She nods slowly.

I can tell she's still scared, but that makes her willingness even more exciting. "I can't wait to kiss your body with my whip. But first, I must undress you."

I slowly lift her t-shirt up over her head and let it fall to the barn floor. I then undo her bra and let it join the shirt on the ground. Her brown nipples are rock hard and difficult to resist.

Moving her hair forward, I "accidently" brush against them as I expose her back. I smile when I hear her soft gasp.

With gentle hands, I guide her to an empty stall at the back of the barn and tell her to grasp the door with her arms spread.

"It's important you do not move."

"Yes," she answers breathlessly.

"Yes, what?" I challenge with a husky growl.

She glances back at me, blushing when she says, "Yes, Master."

My cock swells with desire when I hear Sofia call me by that title. "Good girl," I murmur, lifting her chin and kissing her deeply.

When I pull away, she stares back at me with fear and longing. I must fight not to come in my jeans.

Damn…I'm still such a greenhorn when it comes to

self-control as a Dom. But, in my defense, I am about to introduce a country girl to the world of BDSM—and there's nothing hotter than that.

I unfurl my whip and begin warming up my muscles, being careful not to crack it. I understand now that I need to go slowly as I acclimate Sofia to the idea of being lashed by the bullwhip.

I start by telling her about the hours I've spent perfecting my skill, wanting to assure Sofia that her trust in me is not misplaced.

"Why do you want to whip me?" she asks as she watches the whip fly through the air.

"To unleash my passion on your body."

She moans softly.

Before we begin, I explain, "During our session, I'll be asking your color. You must answer with the word 'green' if you are enjoying it, 'yellow' if it's becoming challenging, and 'red' if you want me to stop."

I stop warming up and move back over to her, whispering huskily, "You are in control, Sofia. Even if I am Master over your body."

She shivers in pleasure.

Kissing her on the neck, I tell her, "I'm about to introduce you to a new level of pleasure."

Stepping back, I take my stance behind her. Sofia looks so tempting with her exposed back, those sexy jean shorts, and her sassy red cowboy boots.

"Whip me," she whispers.

I smile to myself as I deliver the first stroke, licking her with my bullwhip.

"Wow!" she exclaims with a gasp.

"You like?" I growl knowingly.

"I…I never thought it could feel like a whisper."

"Would you like another?"

"Yes, please…Master."

I smile as I give her several more lashes with the same light touch.

She moans in delight.

"Color?"

"Green."

"Would you like to experience what else it can do?"

She hesitates for a moment before answering. "Yes."

I up the pressure of the next stroke and she responds with louder, more passionate, moans.

"Color?"

"Green. I need more."

I have been waiting for this moment. "I will slowly increase the strength of the lashes. Call out 'yellow' when I have reached your limit. I'm counting on you to be vocal."

She turns her head toward me and smiles wickedly. "Oh, I plan to be very vocal."

With that seductive promise ramping up my lust, I begin the erotic task of finding where Sofia's limit lies. I proceed slowly, wanting to build her confidence as I acclimate her body to the bite of my whip.

Soon, her back is a crisscross of light red lashes as she moans with pleasure, unconsciously spreading her legs apart as she begs for more.

It's time to up the ante and see if she is truly a lover of my bullwhip. I let it fly with a lash meant to challenge her.

She gasps and becomes still.

"Color?" I ask.

"I'm excited and scared…" she answers bluntly.

"Another, then?"

"Please, Master."

Oh fuck, she has no idea how hard she's just made my cock.

I grit my teeth, maintaining control over my libido in order to apply the same intensity. I lash her back again and listen with satisfaction to her cry of pleasure.

It stirs my desire, and I suddenly feel the urge to kiss her. Giving into my need, I move over to Sofia, wrapping one arm around her chest just under the swell of her breasts. "Does the bite of the whip excite you?"

"Yes…" she pants, sounding surprised.

I press the coiled whip against her skin, caressing her round ass with it as my other hand slips underneath her shorts. I smile to myself when I feel how wet her pussy is.

Nuzzling her neck, I bite down lightly. "I knew we were kindred spirits, you and I."

She looks at me, her lips begging to be kissed. I claim her mouth, kissing her roughly. I won't last much longer and pull away to deliver the last volley.

I've never felt as turned on as I do now, knowing I have awakened something new inside her.

"Close your eyes and grasp the wood tightly."

I let the whip fly with a more challenging lash, knowing we have almost reached her limit. The girl does me in when she murmurs, "Yellow, but I need more."

I take in a couple of deep breaths to maintain the

precision I need as I deliver the last set of strokes. Sofia lets out a scream of passion that stirs not only me, but the horses as well.

I have no more control left and drop my whip as I advance on her. I turn her head, kissing her deeply. "Are you as turned on as I am?"

"Yes," she whimpers in desperation, rubbing her ass against my erection. I unzip her shorts and pull them down before releasing my aching shaft from the confines of my jeans. Reaching between her legs, I find she is incredibly slick, so I coat the large head of my cock with her excitement.

She grasps my cock, guiding it into her, moaning, "Oh, God, I forgot how huge you are."

"Really?" I ask in a low, seductive tone. "Then let me reintroduce you…"

Knowing now that Sofia has a masochist streak, I challenge her with the length of my cock.

Her vocal screams of satisfaction spur me on, and I begin thrusting into her. It feels too good, and I suddenly stop and pull out.

"No," she whimpers.

"Shh…" I wrap my arm around her front and begin teasing her clit. "You are going to come as I slip that huge cock back inside you."

She nods her head, giving in to the pleasure of my manual stimulation. I keep the head of my cock pressed against her opening, teasing her but not advancing farther as I increase the speed of my fingers.

When I have her squirming and on the edge of orgasm, I thrust into her. Her cry of passion fills the barn, her pussy pulsing around my shaft as she comes.

Having been patient long enough, I give in to my own need and stroke her wet pussy with my massive cock. Edging deeper into her depths, I'm pleased to find her body more receptive to the girth of my shaft after our bullwhip session together.

My balls ache with intense pleasure as I come deep inside her, growling in satisfaction with every thrust. Oh, hell, orgasming has never felt this good…

Afterward, we walk back to the house, my bullwhip in one hand and my other arm wrapped around her to help support her.

Sofia can't stop looking at me.

"What?" I ask with a grin.

"You definitely live up to the title. I'd be willing to call you Master *every* night."

Lost

One of the ranch hands lets Pop know a young calf went missing overnight. The two of us head out on our horses early that the morning to see if we can find her before a predator does. It's an unfortunate aspect of ranching—the loss of cattle to wildlife—but it's to be expected.

I can't blame a hungry carnivore for going after well-fed stock, which is the reason Pop has several Kuvasz herding dogs on the ranch.

The dog breed is known for its mad skills as livestock guardians. The highly intelligent dogs remind me of a cross between a golden retriever and a polar bear. Although they're handsome animals to look at, what makes them ideal for our ranch is that the breed is well known for its unique sense of humor—the perfect fit.

Knowing that Bandit and Kiah are excellent at protecting our herds, I suspect our calf was not attacked in the night but has instead wandered off. Still, time is of the essence if we are going to find her before a mountain lion or a bear comes across her.

Once Pop and I reach the herd, we split up, making ever-growing concentric circles around them, hoping to stumble across her.

After fruitless hours of searching, it seems the calf has vanished into thin air.

Pop shakes his head. "It doesn't make sense. There's no sign of any blood."

"I know. That's got to mean she's still alive."

He shakes his head. "But look how far we've gone out, son. There's no way that calf has wandered this far."

I sigh, not willing to give up on her just yet. Closing my eyes, I still my thoughts as I listen to the breeze rustling through the brush. I feel a call to go west and tell Pop, "Let me look a little longer before we call it quits."

"By all means."

He follows behind me as I head toward the foothills. There's nothing logical about the decision, other than a hunch. As we approach an outcropping of rocks, I dismount and head over to it.

After climbing over several boulders, I find her—a light brown calf the color of a toasted marshmallow. She looks up at me with those sorrowful big brown eyes of hers and cries out, her bloody hind leg wedged in a crack between two rocks.

"It's okay, girl. We're going to get you out…"

I motion to my pop, who dismounts to join me.

"Her hoof is wedged, and she can't move," I inform him.

"Do you want me to head back and get the sledge-hammer?"

"No. I think I can free her if you can hold her still for me."

While my pop positions himself, I take my shirt off and wrap it around the calf's bloody leg, hoping it will provide some extra protection while I work her hoof out of the crack.

She's frightened and struggles in my father's arms, rubbing her hoof against the jagged rocks, making the situation even worse. Needing to do something to calm her down, I start humming a soothing melody. When I feel her start to relax, I slowly wrestle her hoof from the rocks.

I breathe a sigh of relief when the calf's leg is finally free. My pop releases her, but she immediately stumbles and falls onto the rocks, too exhausted by the ordeal to stand up on her own.

I heft her up and, with my father's strong arm steadying me, I make it out of the rock pile and carry her to my mare. I lift the calf up and over my saddle then retie my shirt around her leg so the pressure will stop the bleeding.

The poor animal doesn't stir as I climb on and sit behind her. I guess she's grateful she doesn't have to make the long trek back to the ranch house on her own.

The hot Colorado sun beats down on my naked skin as we head back to the ranch. I've missed the heat of it.

On the ride back, Pop mentions casually, "I've noticed how all the girls seem to flock around you."

I turn toward him and grin.

"While it does a father's heart good to see how well liked you are, it concerns me."

I furrow my brow. "How so, Pop?"

He readjusts his position in the saddle before telling me, "At your age I, too, was on the lookout for a young lass who could encompass the girth of my…substantial need."

A small smile curls the corner of my lip, aware of the meaning behind his carefully worded statement. "Then you understand the struggle."

"I do, son. But I settled down as soon as I found her. The number of young ladies visiting the horse barn since your return has not gone unnoticed by your mother."

I chuckle. "What can I say? You raised a gentleman who knows how to treat a lady right."

"It is one thing to test the waters, and quite another to keep stirring the pot."

I hear a serious undertone in his voice. "Meaning?"

He stops his horse to look me directly in the eye. "There comes a point when you have to open up your heart, son."

Shrugging, I assure him, "I care about each and every one of them."

"But surely, in all of Greeley, you've come across at least one who meets your *unique* requirements."

I nudge Hot Chocolate, and she starts up again, heading home. "I'm only nineteen, Pop."

"Your mother and I got married right out of high school."

"I know."

"And we had you a year later."

I tip my hat to him. "Grateful for it, too."

"I'm not suggesting you marry now. Naturally, we

want you to graduate from college, but…"

I could hear his heartfelt concern. "But what, Pop?"

"I worry that playing the field as enthusiastically as you are, you'll forget the whole point of sex."

I chuckle. "Which is?"

"To express your love for the other person."

I keep my expression calm, but his words stab at my self-confidence. I've never told a soul, but it concerns me that all my girlfriends are just that, friends. Although I thoroughly enjoy their company, I have never been in love with a single one. Heck, all my high school buddies have had at least one crush.

It's made me wonder if I am capable of the kind of relationship my parents have.

My father continues, interrupting my thoughts. "Some men only think with their dicks and miss out on the best thing this world has to offer—the love of a good woman."

"Don't you think this talk is a bit premature? I *just* finished my freshman year in college. There's plenty of time before I need to seriously think about settling down."

"If I were talking to anyone else, I might agree. But I know you, son. The playboy lifestyle you're leading right now will only end in heartache for you."

I huff with amusement. "I've never felt as satisfied with life as I do right now. I'm expanding my knowledge in college *and* enjoying the ladies at the same time. I'd say I'm at the top of my game."

"It's that kind of attitude that concerns your mother and me. We don't want this LA lifestyle to go to your head."

"No worries," I chuckle. "I'll always keep my cowboy roots."

He looks at me skeptically. "I can already see changes in you."

My stubborn streak rears its head on hearing his declaration. Even though I know Pop means well, I'm not about to give up this new world I'm enjoying. I can't imagine my life without the exhilaration of BDSM or the countless subs I have the pleasure of scening with.

No *way* am I ready to give that all up.

Still…I do respect my father, and I want to set his mind at ease. "No need to worry, Pop. I'm planning to take my studies even more seriously from here on out. I'll make something of myself so I can provide for a wife when I'm ready to settle down."

He shakes his head as if my answer displeases him.

It's frustrating. While I connect with the simple way of life here, I'm enjoying my life in California—and I won't give it up, no matter what my pop thinks.

I ride on in silence, but when we finally make it back to the ranch and dismount, I turn to meet his gaze. "Change is inevitable, Pop."

He places his hand on my shoulder. "I don't want you to lose the core of who you are."

I roll my eyes. "That will never happen."

I lower the calf to the ground and Hot Chocolate nudges her lightly in encouragement. I stand back and chuckle to myself.

Would you look at that? It's Hot Chocolate with Marshmallow…

From out of nowhere, Bandit and Kiah race up, barking excitedly as they approach the calf, their tails wagging. It's clear the two are pleased to see the calf safe and sound.

I walk over, patting them both on the head. "She's going to be fine, you two."

Bandit jumps up and puts those massive paws on my chest, almost knocking me over as he licks my face. Before I have a chance to react, he snatches my hat in his teeth and takes off.

"Hey, give that back. You know that's my favorite hat!"

The dog crouches down with his back end in the air, his tail wagging slowly, egging me on to chase him.

When I don't fall for it, he tosses my hat in the air and catches it again in his teeth.

"Don't you dare ruin that hat," I warn him. Walking slowly toward Bandit, I growl under my breath to let him know I'm serious, determined to rescue my hat from those sharp teeth before he can damage it.

He lowers his ears as I approach, lowering his tail before curling it under him in a sign of submission. He looks up at me with guilty eyes.

I reach out to grab my hat from his mouth.

That's when he makes a break for it, wagging his tail as he prances around me like a show horse, my hat still clutched in his mouth.

His name is well earned.

I chase Bandit as he dodges right and left, making a fool of me before Kiah surprises him by snatching it from his mouth.

She gently drops it at my feet.

"Thanks, Kiah." I pat her on the head before picking up my hat and dusting it off.

Glancing at Bandit, I shake my finger at him. "You little bugger…"

The hat is a little wet from his slobber, but no worse for wear. As I place it back on my head, I swear he's laughing at me.

Ma comes out of the house and walks over to us, looking relieved. "You found her!"

"Sure did," Pop answers proudly. "Your son still has a knack for sensing God's creatures."

She smiles at me. "Your connection with them is remarkable, Brad."

I shrug, smiling modestly. "Guess I have to thank you two then, since I was born with the gift."

She takes my hand and squeezes it. "It has everything to do with your big heart, honey. You feel for others, human or animal."

Looking at my bare chest, she teases, "So, I see you're trying to keep up your California tan in Colorado, huh?"

I chuckle, pointing at my shirt wrapped around the calf's leg. "Nah, someone needed it more than I did."

She smiles, looking up at me proudly. "I'm so glad you're back."

"Same here, Ma."

She looks at my pop questioningly.

I know what's going on. She's silently asking him if he has "talked" to me yet, and I watch him answer with an affirmative wink.

I groan inside when I see the same worried look reflected in her eyes. "Not you, too…" I protest.

"Brad, you know I love you, so I'm only going to ask one thing from you."

I'm an idiot to make a promise without knowing what it is, but I love my mother too much to deny her. "What, Ma?"

She places her hand on my chest. "Promise me you'll open yourself up to these girls. I don't want you developing a Teflon heart and letting the right girl slip away."

Leave it to my mother to use a cooking metaphor when it comes to love. "I'll keep that in mind."

"I want more than that. I'm asking you to be open to feeling something deeper for them." She looks lovingly over at my father. "You father is the most open man I've ever met. It's the reason I trusted him with my heart all those years ago." She looks at me again. "I don't expect you to fall in love with all of them, just to be more open with a select few."

"I promise," I assure her.

"Good. You know I only want what's best for you, sweetheart." She stands on tiptoes to give me a kiss on the cheek.

I think it's funny that most parents would advise me *not* to get too serious at my age—but there is nothing typical about my family.

Paige

I sit on the hill that overlooks our family's ranch, hanging out with my three sisters. My mother has sent us off with a picnic basket, insisting we need time together as siblings. I love that about my mother. She has a knack for knowing just what we need, even if we can't figure it out ourselves.

Taking in the warm sun as I eat Ma's magic fried chicken, I sigh in contentment. I suck the meat off one of the wings, savoring my mother's ability to get it perfectly crisp.

Looking at my sisters, I ask, "So, you guys, what's up with Pop? He hasn't played a single practical joke the whole time I've been here."

My sisters glance at one other before the oldest decides to answer. "Pop's worried about you."

"Why? We already had our man-to-man talk."

My little sister looks at me with those big green eyes. "I don't get what's so special about the darn horse barn, Brad. It seems like that's the only place you've been since you came back. Is kissing really better than hanging with us?"

I feel the heat rise in my cheeks. I realize this is her way of letting me know she's missed me. "No, of course not. But my friends really like our horses."

"I bet they do," Ruthie says sarcastically. She's sixteen, so I have no doubt she understands what's really happening in the barn—well, at least part of it.

Megan sighs. "You can't blame Daddy. It's like you're becoming a stranger to us. You used to play jokes on us all the time. Now..." She glances in the direction of the barn.

"So I'll make it a point to make a fool of you more often, sis." I rub the top of her head, adding, "Not that it's hard to do."

She elbows me in the ribs. "You know it's more than that."

"Meaning?"

"Mom and Dad are worried that you are struggling to cope, and I agree."

I frown. "Struggling with what?"

She places her hand lightly on my shoulder. "I don't think you ever got over what happened to Paige."

My throat constricts at the mention of her name. I haven't thought about Paige in years. I shake my head, not wanting to talk about it.

"You two were best friends since you guys were six. You did *everything* together. Remember when Paige collected those cow pies, and you covered them in milk chocolate to sell them on the side of the road?"

I burst out laughing unexpectedly. "Damn, I forgot

about that…"

"The day she died, you stopped talking. I don't think you said a word for months."

A tear almost escapes, but I fight to keep it back. I turn away from her and mumble, "The poor kid was only ten."

"Way too young," my sister agrees.

I shake off the wall of sorrow that threatens to drown me, asking angrily, "What does Paige have to do with any of this?"

"I think you're still hurting, brother."

I snort, shrugging my shoulders. "I was just a kid, and that was more than eight years ago."

She looks at me with compassion. "Paige was an important part of your life, and you lost her."

I snarl. "I don't want to talk about it."

Megan shakes her head. "See what I mean?"

I do *not* like the direction the conversation is going, so I abruptly change it.

Turning to my littlest sister, I grin. "Christina, let's make a date for a tea party. I've been missing drinking tea with you and all your stuffed animal friends."

Her eyes widen. "Really? Because I got three more since you've been gone."

"Only three?"

"Daddy says I have to show restraint."

I chuckle. "Well, I look forward to being introduced to your newest friends."

Turning my attention on Ruthie next, I tell her, "As for you, I'll take you fishing at Barbour Ponds early tomorrow morning." I bump her shoulder. "It's been a while since I strung a worm on a hook."

Ruthie is a tomboy at heart, and seriously skilled with a fishing pole. I've nicknamed her "The Fish Whisperer."

Ruthie giggles, clearly psyched to go fishing with me. "See? I *knew* there was a reason I loved having a big brother."

"What about me?" Megan complains. "You leaving me out?"

"Of course not. I have something extra special planned for you."

"Do tell…"

"You know that roommate of mine?"

"Thane Davis?"

"Yeah, I'm bringing him back with me for Christmas."

A grin spreads across her face. "Does *he* know that?"

"Not yet, but he'll come, don't you worry."

"So, what does that have to do with me?"

"Everything."

She raises an eyebrow. "Spill, big brother."

"I owe the guy and want to surprise him with my best prank yet."

She leans forward with a mischievous glint in her eyes. "Go on."

"He's squeamish about commitment. Like, he has no girlfriends at *all*, so I thought we'd have a little fun with that."

"Oh, I'm liking this so far…"

"I'll take you out for shakes after dinner tonight so we can set up our game plan."

"You've got yourself a deal," she states, that wicked

little mind of hers already contemplating what's ahead.

After the picnic, I tell my sisters to head back to the house without me, explaining, "I'm feeling the need to reconnect with this place."

Megan nods her approval. "I think that's a good idea."

She wraps her arms around her two sisters. "Let's take the basket back to Ma."

I watch them walk off, feeling grateful for my sisters. They ground me in ways no one else can.

Wandering the ranch, I walk for several miles before I see the old cottonwood in the distance. I stop for a moment, realizing my wandering isn't as aimless as I'd first thought.

I reluctantly continue on, my heart beating faster with each step as I approach the huge tree.

This ancient cottonwood has been here for at least a hundred years, and it graces our ranch with its majestic presence. But, that's not the reason the tree holds memories for me.

The massive trunk has a hollow that Paige and I used as a hiding place when we were growing up. I look up at the enormous branches above me and listen as a light breeze rustles the leaves. We both felt an affinity toward the tree, but Paige had a special connection to it, calling it her "old friend."

I'm flooded with memories as I approach the hollow.

Curiosity gets the best of me, and I bend down to reach inside. My heart stops for a second when I feel the bag of marbles.

It was Paige's…

I slide down the trunk of the tree and sit on the ground, my hand trembling slightly as I stare at the small black bag in my hand. We used to spend hours playing marbles here on the hard dirt between the exposed roots.

I open the bag and pour the marbles out, staring at the cat's eyes, aggies, and clearies. The colors are as vibrant as I remember, but it's the peewee steely that catches my eye. That was her most prized possession. She saved up her allowance to buy it.

After the addition of the peewee to her marble collection, she became a fierce competitor whenever we played for keeps.

I pick up the tiny marble, my throat tightening as I remember the innocent joy on her face whenever we played. She always made fish lips and shut one eye just before she sent her marble rolling—her concentration focused entirely on the game. Paige never knew I purposely missed whenever her peewee was at stake. I couldn't bear to win it from her.

I'm surprised by how much that memory crushes my heart, and I shake my head to chase it away. There is the reason I've kept all those memories buried.

Paige did not deserve to die—not like that…

I close my eyes to stave off the rush of grief and nearly jump out of my skin when I feel something cold brush against me.

I open my eyes to see Kiah. She nudges her wet nose

against my cheek and whines softly as she sits down, wagging her white tail slowly in the dirt.

Why she sought me out here is a mystery, but it's clear from the look in those dark brown eyes that she's worried.

I chuckle. "Always looking after your herd, whether animal or human, eh, girl?"

She leans forward to lick my cheek, then noses the marbles in my hand.

I look down at them again and hear Paige's voice.

"I won't be long. Meet you at the park…"

Those were her last words to me. I remember waving to her as she mounted her bike and took off for home to get some change for the ice cream truck.

I waited over a half hour, bummed when the ice cream man came and, after waiting as long as he could, drove off, leaving me there alone.

Once the ice cream truck pulled away, I got on my bike and headed to Paige's house, ready to give her crap for taking so long.

But Paige never made it home.

Some guy backing out of his driveway didn't see her. She flew off the bike on impact, her head hitting the pavement first. I heard later that she'd cried for her mother as she lay dying in the middle of the street.

I still imagine her cries in my head, and it guts me.

Tears blur my vision as I look down at the marbles again. Paige's death killed the child in me. I stopped talking that day, my ten-year-old brain unable to reconcile the immense loss. I refused to attend the funeral service, although my mother begged and pleaded for the sake of her parents.

Recoiling into myself, I blocked out the world, preferring to spend time with the animals. They accepted my silence and asked nothing of me.

I avoided the tree and anything that reminded me of Paige.

In a desperate attempt to escape the weight of her death, I turned my attention on learning how to ride a bull. I needed something that demanded my total focus.

Although my mother was against it at first, Pop understood my need and allowed me to start training. Once I had something to invest my energy in, the words started to flow again—much to my mother's relief.

Being ten, I started with young steers, learning to anticipate their moves. I soon found that each animal had a unique temperament I had to tap into if I wanted to stay on for the required eight seconds.

Bull riding is so much more than gripping with your legs and hanging on for dear life. No, if you strip it down to the essentials, it's a dance between the animal and the man. The bull is the lead, and it's my task to follow every twist, jump, and turn he takes.

Once the gate opens, it's just the animal and me.

The steers I rode didn't care how old I was or why I was there. Their only goal was to get me off their backs, and my only goal was to make it look easy as I kept my free hand up and stayed on until the buzzer sounded.

Eight seconds passes quickly—unless you're on the back of a determined animal.

God, I loved the thrill of it!

But that thrill only lasted so long…

I couldn't bear the lull in between each practice. So, I took up the bullwhip to pass the time. I have to laugh remembering the numerous times I cut myself with my first whip while learning to crack it.

It's a wonder my mother allowed me to continue after the number of times I walked into the kitchen bleeding because of a failed trick. Thankfully, she encouraged me instead of coddling me.

My mother has always been my biggest fan.

I worked hard to escape facing Paige's death, and never once looked back. Now, staring at the marbles in my hand, I realize I wasn't being a coward then—but I am now.

I pat Kiah on the head, knowing what I must do. She licks my hand in encouragement before heading back to the herd.

I slip Paige's prized steely into my jeans pocket before putting the rest of the marbles back in the bag.

It's been more than eight years since I've spoken to Paige's parents, and I hesitate for a second before knocking on their door. Her mother answers, and she immediately puts her hand to her mouth when she sees me. "Brad…"

I take my hat off and nod. "Good afternoon, Mrs. Willis."

"Please come in," she replies graciously, opening the screen door.

I hold my breath before entering Paige's home. It's as if I'm ten again, and I feel as if, at any moment, Paige will round the corner and smile at me.

But she won't—she never will.

As Mrs. Willis leads me into the kitchen, I feel the cold weight of Paige's loss in this place. It hovers over us like a ghost.

"Pa, you won't believe who's come to visit," Mrs. Willis cries excitedly down the hall.

I wait, my anxiety rising, as Mr. Willis slowly makes his way to the kitchen. His face bears the look of a man who has suffered far too deeply.

"You are the last person I expected to see," he says in a guff voice.

I look at him with regret. "Mr. Willis, I'm sorry for not coming to… the funeral." I can't bear to say Paige's name in front of them.

He nods. "Truth be told, if I'd had the choice, I wouldn't have been there, either."

We both swallow down our grief as we stare at each other.

Mrs. Willis breaks the silence by saying, "Please, sit." She points to the kitchen table. "Pardon my bluntness, but why *have* you come today?"

I pull out a chair for her before taking a seat myself. "Mr. and Mrs. Willis, I need to apologize for my silence all these years."

Paige's mother takes my hand in hers. "We understood why, Brad."

"Still, I'm sorry if my actions hurt you in any way."

She pats my hand before getting up and walking over

to an old bookshelf. Pulling out a large photo album, she returns to me with a proud smile. Placing the album on the table, she opens it up.

"We have followed you ever since we lost Paige."

Even though hearing her name is like a physical stab to my heart, I start flipping through the pages. I'm surprised to see clippings of my stints as a young bull rider, along with the awards I earned during my school years. Even my mother doesn't have such an extensive record of my youth.

"When Paige died, I needed something positive to focus on and I found that by following you," she explained.

"How was that helpful?" I ask, not understanding.

She squeezes my hand. "Paige lives in your memories. That makes you precious to us."

Tears come to my eyes. "I miss her."

Both of them nod solemnly.

"That never goes away," Paige's father says in a somber tone.

"I failed…" My voices catches and I have to force the rest of the words out, "…to grieve for her. I couldn't face it."

Her mother smiles, a sympathetic look in her eyes. "But now you are."

I break down in front of them both, ashamed of my lack of control as I start sobbing uncontrollably.

I feel the arms of both of her parents around me as I let out the shock and pain I felt as a young boy after losing my best friend.

They surround me with their presence as we share

our immense grief in silence.

Afterward, I wipe my eyes, apologizing to them. "I came here to comfort you, not to be comforted. I'm sorry."

Mr. Willis nods at me. "Knowing that you still think about Paige brings us comfort, young man. The worst feeling in the world is thinking your child is being forgotten."

Mrs. Willis nods her agreement. "Whether it's healthy or not, we have taken solace in watching you grow into the man you are today. For us—selfishly—it feels like Paige lives on in you."

"She does," I assure her.

Flipping through the book again, Paige's mother highlights events in my life with a look of pride and tenderness I find beautifully heartbreaking. But, when she gets to my failure at the bull riding championship, I look away, thoroughly embarrassed.

"You were so brave taking on that bull. He had quite the reputation in the circuit," Mr. Willis comments.

"I could barely watch," Paige's mother admits to me. "You were so young, and he was so dangerous and massive."

"You two were there?" I asked, shocked to hear it.

"We wouldn't have missed it for the world," her father told me.

"Although I was a nervous wreck…" Mrs. Willis confessed.

I shake my head, feeling embarrassed. "I should have won. I just let my head get in the way."

"An important lesson to learn," Mr. Willis stated.

"Probably more important than winning the championship itself."

"I don't see how." I can still feel the sting of humiliation when Crusher tossed me off his back.

"By not winning, you learned your limitations came from *you*. Not many people learn that—especially at that tender age."

"Still, I would have preferred winning the championship."

Mr. Willis chuckled. "Wouldn't we all?"

Mrs. Willis closes the album slowly with a look of distress. "Unfortunately, after you left for college, I've been unable to add to the book."

I look down at the album, feeling a new connection with Paige's parents. "What if I promise to send you updates in a letter? Would that work?"

"Oh…that would be wonderful!"

I see Mrs. Willis tearing up and regret making her cry as she dabs her eyes. "I'll add anything you send to the album."

She looks at her husband and smiles.

Pulling the bag of marbles from my pocket, I hand them over to Paige's father. "I found them in the old tree hollow and thought you would like to have them back."

I'm moved by his reaction as he reverently takes them from me and opens the bag, pouring the marbles into his hand. His lips become a hard, thin line as he reins in his emotions.

"These were mine as a boy." He glances over at me. "It made me happy that Paige loved playing marbles as much as I did."

"She was a tough cookie to beat," I tell him.

"She definitely took after her father," Mrs. Willis says with a look of motherly pride.

Even after all these years, I'm finding it hard to believe Paige is dead. I wonder if I will ever truly accept it…

"I appreciate you bringing these to us," her father says gruffly, swallowing hard as he stares at the marbles.

I remember the peewee in my pocket and dig it out to give to him. "There's one more."

"Oh, no, you keep it. Paige would want you to have that one," he tells me.

Tears prick my eyes. "Thank you, Mr. Willis."

He puts his hand on my shoulder, grasping it tightly. "Means a lot, you visiting us today."

I bow my head in shame. "I know it was a long time in coming, sir."

"You came when you were ready. That's all that matters," Mrs. Willis assures me with a gentle smile.

"I won't be a stranger," I promise them both as I stand up to leave.

Mr. Willis stops me for a moment and says solemnly, "You'll always have a place at our table, Brad."

I can't express how much that means to me and shake his hand firmly in gratitude before giving Mrs. Willis a hug.

I can definitely feel Paige's spirit in this place. Instead of it making me feel uncomfortable, it fills me with a sad peace, and I call out silently as I leave:

Goodbye, Paige…

New Possibilities

I return to LA to begin my sophomore year with a feeling of renewed confidence. I'm more driven than ever, but now I'm also grounded because of my family.

Remembering my promise to my mother, I'm even entertaining the idea that this could be the year I finally experience what it feels like to fall in love.

It could happen…

I begin unpacking all the things I kept in storage, grateful for the extra space, as well as the private bathroom in this bigger dorm room. I know the ladies I invite over will certainly appreciate it.

After a full day of hauling crap up to the third floor, I'm ready to take a break. Folding my arms behind my head, I lay on my bed, surprised that Davis hasn't made an appearance yet.

I haven't heard boo from the guy since I split to head home for the summer.

Thane doesn't show up until late that afternoon. He's carrying a single suitcase, a duffle bag slung over his shoulder, and his collection of suits. Apparently, some things never change.

Standing up, I grasp the hand he holds out to me.

"Good to see you again, Anderson."

I give Thane a solid handshake before pulling him in for a manly hug. "Likewise, buddy."

Although Thane stiffens, he slaps me on the back before letting go.

I stare at his utter lack of furnishings. "Planning on living like a monk again this year?"

He shrugs, glancing at my fully equipped living space. "I really don't see the need to pamper myself like some people I know."

"Hey, the ladies love a man who can pamper them," I chuckle.

Holding up his duffle bag, he says confidently, "I have everything I need in here to pamper them."

I realize he's assembled a toy bag for the dungeon over summer break, and it gets me thinking.

"So, I gotta know what you did while I was gone."

"Spent most of the summer helping to remodel my uncle's house."

"Sure, you did…" I tell him, not believing Thane for one second.

"I'm serious." He then adds with a smile, "However, I *did* spend several memorable weekends out at Durov's beach house."

"I suspected as much."

"How about you? Did the quiet country life drive you batty?"

"Not at all. In fact, it turns out cowgirls enjoy the

kinkster lifestyle."

He raises his eyebrows. "You're telling me you introduced that quiet town of Greeley to your perverted ways?"

"I did. Not only that, but I told my ma all about you."

"Why would you do that?"

"She wanted to know," I say with a shrug. "Naturally, she's insisting you come up for Christmas break."

"Right…" Thane laughs.

"I'm serious, buddy. My mother has already started planning what she'll cook when you're there."

"That's crazy."

"Hey, any friend of mine is a part of our extended family," I tell him with a grin. "I think she's hoping to impress you."

He scoffs at my assertion. "There's no need for her to go to all that trouble."

I wrap my arm around his shoulder. "My mama takes hospitality *very* seriously."

Davis chuckles, shaking his head. "Can you really imagine me fitting in with a bunch of country folk?" When I frown, he adds, "No offense. I just think they would find me a little 'stiff' for their liking."

"Everyone finds you a little stiff, buddy. That's part of your unique charm."

He laughs, setting his lone suitcase on his bed.

"So, you'll come, then?" I prod as he starts to unpack.

"Where?"

"To visit my parents for Christmas?"

"It's not my thing—the whole family gathering over the holidays."

"Come on. You wouldn't want to break my poor Ma's heart, would you?" I reach over and grab the tin from my desk, handing it to him. "She even made you a special batch of chocolate chip cookies to celebrate your sophomore year."

Davis opens the lid and takes in a whiff of the chocolaty goodness inside. I see that smile he's trying to hide.

"I suppose not…" he answers.

"Good, 'cause I can't stand to see my mother cry." I give him a nudge with my elbow.

Little does Davis know he's just fallen headfirst into my trap!

"I'm heading to the dungeon in a few. You coming with me?" Davis asks me later that night.

I glance up from my textbook, looking at him strangely. "Wait. Didn't you spend the entire first week going over every textbook you had so you were prepared for the semester?"

He shrugs. "Seems like a waste of time, since most of my professors failed to utilize the course textbooks."

I stare at him—open-mouthed. "Who are you?"

"What do you mean?"

"I came back wanting to emulate you this semester, and you want to go play at the dungeon instead? Seriously, man, what's happened to you while I was gone?"

He smirks, looking amused. "I'm still on a path to graduate a year early. However, I'm determined to be more efficient about it this year."

I slam my book closed. "Well, hell, that sounds like a solid plan to me."

Changing into my dungeon gear, I grab my bullwhip, and tell him, "I've got to admit, as entertaining as it was introducing the ladies to my bullwhip, I've been hankering to get back to the dungeon for some serious fun."

"You might notice some changes there."

Now he's got my attention. "Like what?"

"There was a bit of a shakeup over the summer. Egos got involved and people left."

"Don't tell me Durov shot his mouth off and got himself banned?"

"No, but several of his friends are no longer there."

"Damn…" I shake my head, surprised by the news. "What the hell happened?"

"Some prominent members wanted to expand the dungeon, but the majority insisted on keeping it intimate."

"And you?"

"Hey, I'm still a newbie there, so I didn't voice an opinion—which turned out to be wise because the discussion got pretty heated. Unfortunately, things were said that couldn't be taken back and lines were drawn."

"How many members did the dungeon lose?"

"Five Doms and three subs."

"That's a huge hit for the group."

"It is, and you can feel it in the dungeon. It's made

the place feel a lot more subdued."

I shake my head sadly. "Damn."

"But, now that you're back, I'm sure you'll liven up the place." He smacks me on the back. "You have that effect on people."

"Hey, whatever I can do to help," I say with a grin.

Thane wasn't kidding about the change in the dungeon. When we arrive, the Doms look at me with suspicion. They still consider me a newcomer and possible threat to the secrecy of the group, but I meet each of their gazes with a confident tip of my hat.

I'm not about to get dragged into the drama that ripped the group apart. As far as I'm concerned, by keeping the dungeon small, the powers that be are ensuring no riffraff get in and spoil all our fun.

Unfortunately, all it would take is for one person to say the wrong thing at the wrong time, and the entire dungeon could disappear. I've heard of it happening to other groups in the area.

The authorities clearly don't understand the dynamics of a D/s relationship, mistaking it for abuse rather than consensual play.

There is real risk in being a Dom.

I glance around, looking for familiar faces, and am relieved when I spy glee, the little pixie with ash brown hair and those sparkling doe eyes. But she doesn't seem her usual spunky self, so I head over to find out why.

"Been too long, little lady," I tell her as I approach.

Glee looks up and smiles, but her eyes are tinged with sorrow. I don't even need to ask why, because I can see she's no longer wearing a collar.

Rather than question her on it, I sit down beside her. "I must say I'm glad to see you're still here. The dungeon would be bleak without you."

Her eyes soften as she looks at me. "You are kind to say so."

I've always had an interest in glee, but I also respected the collar she wore. Now that it's gone, all bets are off. However, she is obviously hurting and doesn't need some fool trying to sweep her off her feet at the moment.

Sighing deeply, she looks around the dungeon. "I like playing here, but now I feel out of place."

I shake my head. "Nope, you're exactly where you belong. Why would you even question that?"

"My Master ordered me to leave with him, but I couldn't go…" Her chin trembles. "He said it was either Him or the dungeon." She looks at me with tearful eyes. "But this is the only place I feel safe and accepted."

"I personally don't understand why he left, but putting you in that position wasn't exactly fair."

"I couldn't handle the idea of never being here with my friends, including you, Master Anderson." She looks around sadly. "But now, I feel…lost."

"While I can appreciate the pain of losing that partnership, I assure you that you will be well taken care of here. And I, for one, am glad you chose to stay."

She gives me a slight smile, but the sadness remains.

My heart goes out to her, so I ask, "Although this may seem a little forward, would you care for a little scene with my bullwhip?"

Her eyes flash with relief. "That would be deeply appreciated. In fact, I would love it if you would challenge me. I'm in need of a serious challenge right now."

I hold my hand out to glee and walk her to the center area. I want everyone to admire this girl who has given up her collar to stay here among us.

I secure her wrists in the cuffs and pull the chains above taut so that her movement is limited.

Glee has stated she wants to be challenged, and I'm familiar with her level of experience. After a summer of introducing vanilla girls to my whip, I can finally let my whip fly the way it's meant to.

I lean forward and whisper in her ear, "I will not be interrupting the scene to check in, so call out your safeword if I push you too hard."

The look she gives me is not one of fear but of gratitude. I can tell this isn't just a pleasure session for glee; she needs the power behind this exchange.

Wanting to create a dramatic start to our scene, I pull a butterfly knife from my bag and approach her with hungry eyes. Flicking it open, I grab her t-shirt and cut into it with my knife.

She gasps as I rip it down, exposing her smooth skin. I make short work of her shirt and then go for her bra next, leaving her chest completely exposed to me. Her nipples are hard and her breathing shallow. Both tells me she finds my rough treatment exciting.

But I'm not done yet.

Closing the butterfly knife with a flourish, I slip it into my pocket. Needing more of her skin exposed, I go down on one knee to pull her mini skirt and panties off in one swift motion. As I look up at her, I slowly trail my fingers up her inner thigh, barely`brushing against her pussy.

She bites her lip, looking at me longingly.

Before I stand back up, I lean forward and press my lips against the peach fuzz of her trimmed mound, listening with satisfaction when she lets out a soft moan.

I like to start out tenderly whenever a sub is about to experience the true intensity of my whip—I enjoy building the anticipation as she waits for that first painful bite.

Standing up, I hover over glee's tiny frame.

Tilting her chin up, I give glee a slow, sensual kiss— drawing it out so every fiber of her being is focused on me. She sighs when I break the embrace.

I savor this moment between a Dom and sub.

Glee's complete surrender to my bullwhip has an erotic power that acts much like an aphrodisiac for me.

My cock stirs with desire as I prepare to lash her with my bullwhip. I move behind her with purposeful steps, noting that several subs are now watching our exchange.

Reaching into my bag, I pull out my beloved whip. Unlike Myrtle, this one has no name because it's an extension of me.

I let it unfurl, smiling to myself as I send it flying through the air to warm up. The subs who were watching from a distance now move in a little closer. It seems they have been missing my brand of kink.

While I certainly don't mind having an audience, I won't allow it to become a distraction. The sub before me is my sole focus.

"Glee, I am honoring your request to be challenged.

Are you ready?"

"Oh, yes, Master. Please…" she begs breathlessly.

Like the kiss, I begin by giving her a gentle caress with my whip. She giggles in surprise.

As her Master for this session, I exude confidence in my skill and the ability to bring her what she has requested. Inside, I am lusting with desire, hungry to provide her with the challenge she is begging for.

I crack my whip several times to alert the entire dungeon of my intention.

I then stare at glee's naked body, the sensual curve of her back calling to me. With focused precision, I deliver the first challenging stroke. The skin on her back ripples from the impact and her loud gasp fills the air.

I warm up her skin with several more equally challenging lashes and note when she begins to relax, as she grows used to them.

Upping the power behind the strokes, I challenge her again with a volley of lashes. She starts moaning but does not call out her safeword.

Once I see her body growing used to the higher intensity, I increase it again.

This time, the dungeon is filled with her cries. She still does not use her safeword, although it is obvious the strength of my strokes is pushing her body to its limits.

Glee's back is covered by the red stripes of my whip. So, I change things up a little, delivering a few choice strokes across her ass.

She squeals, making several Doms around me chuckle.

That's when I crack the whip just behind her neck.

She cries out in terror, even though the whip doesn't touch her.

I smile to myself as I return to her back, delivering strokes that are guaranteed to test her.

Glee trembles in her bonds, a stream of tears running down her face. But, rather than a look of pain, she wears a calm expression. I can tell I've hit a point of harmony and no longer increase the strength of my lashes.

I keep her in that heightened state until I've determined she's had enough.

Once the whip stops flying, I hear the soft sounds of her crying. Normally, a woman's tears bring me pain. In this case, however, it is a sign of a job well done.

Coiling the whip, I attach it to my belt before walking to her. Glee's head is down, sweat dripping from her skin.

I lift her head up and smile. "Are you satisfied, darlin'?"

At first, she nods slowly, then starts shaking her head.

"What more do you need?"

"You, Master. I need you."

Her desire increases my own, and I lean down, whispering, "Why don't we retire to one of the back rooms so I can satisfy you *fully*?"

With one arm wrapped securely around her torso, I unbuckle her wrist restraints and she falls like a rag doll into my waiting arms. Taking her hands, I wrap them around the back of my neck. "Hold onto me."

Hoisting her small frame up, she wraps her legs around my waist, and I walk off the main area to find a secluded room for us.

Once there, I lay her face down on the bed.

Joining her, I examine her marks as I lightly graze them with my fingers.

She purrs in response. "I really needed that."

"I did, too."

I lean forward and kiss her on the lips.

Glee smiles at me in adoration. "I was so torn up about what happened, but now I feel like cotton candy."

"Cotton candy?" I chuckle.

"Yeah…all fluffy inside."

"What does fluffy feel like?" I ask, as I reach between her legs. Glee is impressively wet. "You really *do* like being challenged, don't you?"

Gazing into my eyes, she answers, "You found the perfect balance of pleasure and pain. I could have continued for hours."

I chuckle at her claim. "It's a good thing I understand your body's limits, or you could have gotten yourself in trouble, young lady."

Her eyes sparkle with desire as she looks down, licking her lips seductively. "Nothing completes an intense scene better than deep penetration."

"So, it's my cock you're needing, is it?" I ask, teasing her clit with light brushes of my finger.

She presses her pussy against my hand. "Yes…that huge cock will be my salvation."

I smirk, appreciating her sentiment.

Knowing she is still flying high from the session, and is physically weakened by it, I adjust her position so she is kneeling beside the bed with her stomach resting against the mattress—doggie style. A preferred position of mine.

I make quick work of my clothes, but I ask glee for her preference. "Hat on or off?"

"Oh, definitely on. I *want* to be ridden, cowboy."

I kneel behind her, stroking my cock as I spread her outer lips with my fingers to get a better view of her hot pussy. "Hold on, little filly. This cowboy is about to make all your dreams come true."

Coating my cock with her sexual excitement, I ease my large shaft into her. Glee wiggles her hips, moaning lustfully as my shaft slowly slips inside.

"Wow, your pussy is ready for a pounding," I state in admiration. Normally, I would have to spend a while warming her body up to take the girth of my shaft, but something about our session today has gotten her loose and primed.

Grasping her hips with both hands, I watch as I sink my massive cock deeper into her. It is still a challenge for her body to take it all, but she purrs in pleasure. "Fuck me, Master."

Oh, hell…all my restraint disappears as I pull back before thrusting harder.

Glee lets out a scream of pleasure, pressing her fine little ass against me, wanting to take even more.

Both of us are riding the high of our shared scene and, as a result, my senses are heightened as I claim her body with my cock. I feel everything—the heat of her pussy, the tight constriction, and her slick inner walls inviting me to ravage her.

Every cry from glee's lips sends bursts of shivers

down my spine. Gripping her ass, I close my eyes and stroke her more deeply. When she starts making quick little gasps, I pause for a moment and feel her pussy tense.

She's on the brink of an orgasm and I want to feel it. "You have my permission to come."

I groan in satisfaction as her pussy pulses around my thick shaft. But, before her orgasm ends, I begin thrusting again.

Glee lets out a cry of surprise but quickly matches my rhythm, encouraging me to fuck her harder.

At this point, I *need* to come inside her.

Smacking her hard on the ass, I tell her to hold on tight. Taking advantage of her insatiable need, I give her all of me and revel in the sound of glee's passionate cries as I release my come deep inside her pussy, filling her with my seed as I roar in primal satisfaction.

Afterward, I wrap my arms around her, pulling her against me. "Satisfied, darlin'?" I murmur.

"Yes…I don't think I'll be able to walk for a week."

I chuckle into her hair. "I do like a girl with a bow-legged walk."

Picking her up, I lay her back on the bed and curl up beside her.

"Master Anderson," she says, a hint of hesitancy in her tone. "I wasn't sure I'd made the right decision to stay, until now. I wouldn't have missed this experience for the world."

I run my thumb against her sweaty cheek as I look at her tenderly. "I wouldn't have either, glee."

The genuine smile she gives me lightens my heart.

Squeezing her tight, I sigh in contentment. Glee is one of a kind. I could almost envision a future with her.

I know she has several Doms at the dungeon she's extremely close to, including the Russian, but maybe she's worth causing a few waves…

Testing the Waters

Thane and I meet the Russian for lunch at my favorite off-campus diner. The two of us arrive there a few minutes early and stand outside, waiting for Durov to show up.

After fifteen minutes, I give up and go inside to sit at the counter, telling Thane, "This stomach waits for no man."

"I can't blame you. I'm starving, too."

As I'm looking over the menu trying to decide what sides I'm adding to my chicken and waffles, I suddenly find myself in a chokehold.

I growl as I grab the man's muscular arm and wrestle with him until I break free. When I turn to face my attacker, I see Durov is standing there, wearing a shit-eating grin on his face.

"Good to see you again, cattleman."

"What's with the choke hold, Durov?" I grumble, grabbing the glass of water in front of me to calm my need to punch him in front of all the other diners.

"Being late to lunch is considered rude where I come from." Durov points to a table in the corner. "I have been sitting there for fifteen minutes waiting for my rude American friends to arrive."

"We were at least ten minutes early," I correct him. "But we were waiting outside for a pompous Russian."

"We were," Thane agrees with a smirk.

One of the waitresses rushes up with a worried expression. "Is everything okay here, gentlemen?"

Durov turns to her and smiles, amping up his Russian charm. "*Da.* As you can see, my delinquent friends have finally arrived so I'd like to order some food."

She blushes as she pulls out her pad. "Of course! What would you like, Mr. Rytsar?"

"Just Rytsar to you," he says intimately, giving her a private wink.

If he hasn't already brought her over to the dark side, I have no doubt he soon will.

When we sit down at the table, after she's taken our orders, I chastise him. "Have you no shame? That poor woman has no idea that behind that Russian accent lays a wicked soul."

He smirks. "You'd be surprised how many women prefer wicked souls."

The waitress quickly returns with drinks for all of us and complementary fries for Durov. "Since your friends were late, I thought these might tide you over until your meal arrives."

"You are far too generous," he states, grabbing a French fry and taking a bite as he stares at her intently.

Thane nudges him in the ribs, whispering in a low

voice, "It's a family restaurant, so cool it before you get us kicked out." He nods toward the cook, who is standing with his arms crossed, spatula in one hand, his eyes glued on Durov.

The Russian nods at the cook as if they are longtime friends.

Wanting to end the staring match between Durov and the cook, I ask, "So, I hear good times were had at the beach house over the summer."

"Indeed, they were," Durov replies with a mysterious grin. "However, I am not at liberty to go into detail." He leans toward me and asks in a low voice, "I am curious about how your country girls in Colorado reacted to your newfound talent."

I smile with a sense of pride as I lean back in my chair. "Let's just say a good time was had by all."

He looks at me with admiration. "If anyone can tame a vanilla girl, it's you."

I'm not sure if his comment is meant as an insult or an actual compliment. So, I look at Thane.

He nods in agreement. "You have a knack for winning a person over to your side. I've experienced it myself."

I snatch a handful of Durov's fries and stuff them in my mouth. Still chewing, I mumble, "So, I noticed glee is no longer collared."

Durov gazes at me intently. "*Nyet*, she is not."

"Just wondering if you have set your sights on her."

The Russian gives me a knowing grin. "Why do you ask?"

"I'm simply curious."

"Of course, you are," he says, winking at Thane before he answers my question. "I have no designs on the girl."

I turn to Thane. "Are you continuing your lessons with Samantha now that school is back in session?"

He gives me the same knowing smile. "I am."

"And I take it glee will be involved?"

"That's been the plan all along."

"Good…" I reply nonchalantly, taking a sip of my soda.

Thankfully, our food arrives, and for the next several minutes we focus on satisfying our empty stomachs, eating our meals in silence.

I glance at the table across the diner. "Hey, buddy. Remember that family who sat there the last time we ate here?"

"Oh, yeah.," Thane laughs. "That father kept staring at me with daggers in his eyes."

I nod, chuckling. "Yeah, the dude seemed to have serious issues with you, but the kid was cute—"

Durov interrupts me, blurting, "Out with it, cattleman. Are you seeking to claim glee for yourself?"

I actually blush, hearing him state it so bluntly. "Not exactly."

"What, then?" Thane asks, clearly interested.

"I'm not trying to mess with your plans or anything. I understand she likes to scene with other Doms and has a working relationship with you, Thane. It's just that…I like glee a lot."

The Russian breaks out in laughter.

I feel a surge of anger and scowl at him. "It's nothing

to laugh about."

"I am not laughing at you. I'm laughing at us."

"Meaning?"

When Durov doesn't answer immediately, Thane speaks up. "Durov is struggling with his growing feelings for Samantha."

Holy hell.

I'd totally forgotten about the instant attraction he'd had for her that first meeting just before I left for summer break.

"Do tell," I encourage Thane.

"Well—"

Durov interrupts. "If you explain your feelings toward glee, I will share mine."

The Russian is normally very aloof, so this is unexpected offer is something I can't refuse.

Before I say anything, however, I tell them, "This stays between us."

"Of course," Durov answers, hitting himself on the chest three times in a gesture of solidarity.

"I pledge my silence," Thane agrees amiably.

Assured of their loyalty, I decide to be completely open. "I've liked glee for a while. I mean, who doesn't? But seeing her without the collar has done something to me."

"Are you falling in love?" Durov asks.

"No, but…I feel there could be potential, and I haven't felt that way before. To be honest, it scares me a little."

"Go on," Durov states, leaning in closer, obviously intrigued.

"I've never been one to fall for a girl. But something my Ma said this summer has been playing in my head, and it got me thinking differently when I saw glee was no longer collared."

"If you pursue her, will you expect exclusivity?" Thane asks.

I shake my head. "I couldn't imagine glee going for that. I'm not sure how it would work, really."

"It would be important to iron that out with her," Thane states. "I never fully understood the dynamic glee had with her former Master, and I wonder...seeing how you and I are friends, if you'll be okay with me scening with your collared sub. Even if it *is* for educational purposes."

"It seems premature for me to answer that," I reply, chuckling. "I haven't even asked the poor girl out yet."

"I believe you *should* think about it," Thane urges. "It's imperative you understand your own hard limits before approaching her."

"Wise counsel," Durov states.

I nod to the Russian and chuckle, knowing Thane dislikes being called wise—but the kid really is a fountain of uncommon wisdom.

The Russian looks me in the eyes, saying, "I'm far more interested in your feelings toward the girl. You stated that it scared you."

I smile nervously. "Yeah, you know...it's unsettling to feel overly attracted to a person."

"I *do* know," he states.

With that opening, I decide to dig deeper. "So, things are getting serious between you and Samantha, huh?"

"*Nyet*," he states vehemently.

Thane smirks. "Let's just say that Durov isn't sure what he's feeling toward her."

I nod to the Russian. "Whatever it is, it's got you feeling uneasy."

"*Da!*" he says, pointing at me as if I'm a genius or something.

"What do you plan to do about it?" I ask him.

He raises his hands in the air and shouts, "I don't know!" His yell draws the attention of all the tables around us.

While Thane pats him on the shoulder to calm him down, I smile at a table full of construction workers who are staring hostilely at Durov.

"Woman troubles," I explain.

They all nod, chuckling amongst themselves as they go back to their meal.

"It's a universal problem," I tell Durov.

Looking at Thane with a raised eyebrow, I add, "Except for *certain* people."

Thane only smiles. "Take my advice. Emotions invite too many variables."

"Sometimes you do not have a choice, comrade," Durov huffs.

Thane seems amused by his statement. "Can't get Samantha out of your mind?"

"I cannot. It makes no sense to me. When we are apart, I drive myself crazy thinking about her, and when we are together…my only thought is to possess her." He looks at us. "But she is not a woman to be possessed. What sorcery is this?"

"Sounds like love to me," I tell him.

He shakes his head. "*Nyet.* This cannot be love but, if it is not, I don't know *what* it is. That's why I wanted to talk to you. To hear your own experience and compare it with mine."

"Sorry to disappoint you, but I'm not in as deep as you are."

He leans close and says confidently. "But you will be."

I snort in amusement. "How can you be so sure?"

"You are easy to read. It's the reason vanillas trust you so completely."

"You say that as if it is a bad thing."

"Not at all. But is does make it easy for me to understand now you tick."

I turn to Thane, not liking the Russian's assertion. "Is he full of crap or what?"

Thane answers amiably, "You are a genuine soul. It's a rarity."

"So, you are agreeing with him that I'm an open book?"

Thane looks at me with compassion. "I personally think it's an asset few people possess."

"Asset my ass." I look around apologetically at the families eating around us.

I silently vow, then and there, to start working on being more guarded. I don't like the idea that other Doms can read me so damn easily.

"So, Anderson, you have a chance to walk away from glee right now, before things get muddy. Will you?" Durov asks.

I snort. "Why would I do that?"

"Exactly! That's what I thought going in. I ignored my fears and walked in blindly."

"Are you suggesting I skip the whole glee thing? Is that it?"

"*Nyet.* You're the only one who can possibly understand what I'm going through. I'll need any advice you can offer."

I finish up the last bite of my waffle, chuckling to myself. I never thought Durov would actively encourage me to pursue glee.

As we head out, Durov stops to pay the bill. He gives the waitress a generous tip and adds an extra five. "Give this to your cook and tell him he needs to smile more."

I shake my head as we walk out, amused by his nerve.

This little gathering has been quite productive for me. I see no reason not to ask glee out. But, unlike the poor Russian, I have no intention of diving in too deep.

One simple date.

That's all I need.

The Seduction

Now that I have the green light, I make plans to win glee over. Grounded in my country roots, I decide to do it the old-fashioned way—with flowers and an invitation to dinner.

It seems incongruous, given the atmosphere of the dungeon, but I'm about to stake my claim, and I want all the other Doms there to be aware.

I hear the buzz start when I enter the dungeon with a simple bouquet of flowers in my hand.

Some of the Doms start nudging each other as I walk in confidently. I hear the excited twitters of several subs mix in with the deep-throated snickers of my peers. I feel badly when several of the girls look up at me expectantly and then pout when I pass by them.

I see glee talking to a Dom on the other side of the dungeon. It must be an intense discussion, because she's completely unaware when I come up beside her.

"Glee, may I speak with you for a moment?"

She turns with a smile on her face, but her eyes widen when she notices the flowers in my hand. "Of course, Master Anderson."

Her gaze remains focused on the bouquet when she asks, "What are those for? Sensation play?"

I chuckle, amused by the fact that her thoughts immediately turn to BDSM.

"Actually, they're for you." I hold the flowers out to her. "I would like to formally ask you out on a date."

I hear little gasps from the other subs and a low growl from the Dom she was just talking to.

She stares at the flowers for a moment before looking up at me in surprise. "A date?"

"Yes. I would like to take you out to a nice dinner and get to know you on a more personal level."

Her pink lips curve into a shy smile. "A vanilla date?"

"Yes."

She glances around the dungeon, blushing. The dungeon has grown so quiet, you can hear a pin drop.

I notice the Dom who was talking to her shaking his head when she gazes over at him, and I suddenly feel sick wondering if I'm about to be shot down in front of the entire assembly.

Oh, well… You either go big or go home.

I attempt to win her over with a charming smile. "It's totally up to you, darlin'."

"Do you know how long it's been since I've gone on a vanilla date?"

I reach out and graze her cheek with my hand. "Far too long, I reckon."

She giggles softly.

Glee looks around the room again as she decides my

fate, but when her gaze returns to me, I read her answer in her light blue eyes.

"You're right." Taking the flowers from me, she brings them to her nose and takes in their scent. "Master Anderson, they smell divine! I adore the scent of freesia."

"Good," I grin. "I plan to pick you up at seven tomorrow evening, if that works for you."

"Tomorrow?"

I tilt my head. "Is that a problem?"

She graces me with a bashful smile. "No."

I wink. "Then I'll see you at seven, glee."

As I turn to leave, she calls after me. "Master Anderson?"

I turn back to face her, wondering if she is suddenly having second thoughts. "Yes?"

"What should I wear?"

"Whatever makes you happy, darlin'." I tip my hat to her.

She grins, looking at her flowers again.

I walk away, nodding to the other Doms as I leave the dungeon, happy to have staked my claim.

I dress up for our date—my best jeans, a white button-down shirt, leather vest, snakeskin boots, and my favorite Stetson.

Five minutes before seven, I arrive at the house she rents with four other girls. The instant I knock on the door, I hear a burst of giggles on the other side.

When glee answers the door, I let out a long, appreciative whistle. I'm used to seeing her in black leather or vinyl, but tonight she's wearing a yellow summer dress. It gives her a sweet, but flirty appearance.

Glee looks me over with an admiring gaze. "I didn't think you could get any more handsome, Master Anderson."

"You can call me, Brad," I inform her.

The girls behind her twitter and I glance in their direction. I recognize several of them because I have scened with them at the dungeon. The girls immediately quiet down and lower their gaze out of respect to me, as is customary for the dungeon.

However, I notice they keep taking quick peeks, wanting to satisfy their curiosity.

Navigating the vanilla world outside the parameters of the dungeon is proving interesting for us all.

Glee bites her lip, looking at me nervously. "I'm not sure I can call you Brad…I'm so used to calling you Master."

I give her a wink. "Why don't you give it a try?"

"Okay, umm…Brad." She blushes profusely after saying my name.

"Now, that wasn't so hard, was it?"

She giggles.

I find glee's sudden shyness charming. "How would you prefer I address you this evening?"

Her eyes grow wide. "I…" She looks down at her feet for a moment before meeting my gaze. "My given name is Deanna."

I tip my hat. "Are you ready to go, Miss Deanna?"

She bites her lip again and turns toward her friends. "Bye, guys," she squeaks, quickly shutting the door behind her.

She's obviously nervous, which I find amusing. Who knew a vanilla date could unbalance an experienced sub like glee?

I hold out my arm to her. When she takes it, she smiles up at me bashfully with those beautiful doe eyes of hers.

It surprises me that this attractive woman seems unused to having a man take her out purely for the pleasure of her company. The fact that we initially met in the dungeon does make this first date slightly awkward.

We know each other on a physical basis, but not on a personal one—at least, not yet.

When I notice glee averting her gaze, I realize I need to address what my expectations are for the evening. "Deanna…"

Her head pops up as if she's surprised to hear her name from my lips. "Yes, Mast—Brad?"

"I want you to pretend we've just met. Forget all protocol. I want you to treat me like you would any man you met outside the BDSM community."

Her eyes grow wide. "But I'm afraid I might accidently offend you."

"The only way I'll be offended is if you treat me like your Master and not your date."

"Now the pressure's really on…" she giggles nervously.

"You do realize how crazy this sounds? You, the

sweet little masochist, intimidated by a vanilla date?"

She breaks out in laughter, nodding her agreement. "It's like the opposite of the rest of the world."

"It is." I grin. "Tonight, I'm looking for a simple night out. I want to enjoy a good meal and meaningful conversations. I have no other expectations, other than that."

She shakes her head, smiling. "Why are you doing all this?"

"I was sincere when I said I wanted to connect with you on a different level—to get to know the Deanna behind the glee, so to speak."

Her eyes sparkle. "I actually find that…refreshing."

"I do, too," I agree as I start the car. I have to admit, there's a feeling of inner excitement I've never experienced on a date before. It definitely bodes well for the night ahead.

I take her to a highly rated steakhouse, and watch with satisfaction as she takes me up on my offer to order anything she wants off the menu. When the huge lobster comes out with her filet mignon, she giggles.

"What's so funny?"

She places her napkin in her lap and looks at me sheepishly. "I think I may have ordered *way* too much. I'm sorry."

"Darlin', as long as you ordered what you wanted, that's all that matters. How much you eat is irrelevant to me."

Picking up her fork and knife, she looks at her plate hungrily. "Well, I definitely did that, and these leftovers are going to make my girlfriends super jealous."

I chuckle to myself when I hear her moan in ecstasy when she takes her first bite. I personally take pleasure watching a woman enjoy her food.

It gives me a thrill I can't explain.

Although this restaurant is a good one, I look forward to the day when I have my own place and cook for myself.

Our dinner conversation starts off light, but I quickly delve into what makes this woman tick. "What's something you're passionate about?"

"Besides BDSM?"

"Yes."

"Travel. Someday, I hope to travel the world. And not with a tour guide. No, I want to fully experience each place I visit. I want to eat where the locals eat and immerse myself in their music and culture."

I find her answer intriguing. "Where have you been so far?"

Glee blushes. "Nowhere, actually. I don't have the money, but that's my dream."

"Travel is a worthy endeavor."

"How about you, Brad? What's a passion of yours?"

"Gardening."

She laughs. "Really?" She studies my face as if she doesn't believe me. "I never imagined you were the gardening type."

I grin when I tell her, "I prefer to garden in the nude."

Her jaw drops momentarily, then her eyes sparkle with amusement. "Well now, that sounds like fun."

"It's very freeing."

"I bet," she grins before taking another bite of her lobster. "I've never been much into plants but thinking of you gardening naked sounds like a lot of fun to me."

"I did notice your house is seriously lacking garden beds and I'm not opposed to remedying that situation for you."

"Oh, the girls and I would be happy to help, but I'm not sure what the neighbors would think."

"Only one way to find out," I say, winking at her. She is definitely an easy girl to like. "So, Deanna, we seem pretty compatible. Wouldn't you agree?"

"I do."

"Just like any couple dating, I figure we'll just have to see where this leads."

"But…" she hesitates for a moment before continuing. "Brad, I really liked the arrangement I had with my previous Master. He took pride in sharing me with Dominants he respected, and I loved all the attention and new experiences that came from those exchanges." She sighs nervously before adding, "I don't want to give that up."

I nod. "I suspected as much."

She bites her lip. "To be brutally honest, I don't think you would be able to handle an open relationship like that."

I frown slightly. "Well, to be equally as blunt, I'm unsure as well. However, I like you, Deanna. And I'm willing to try."

She looks at me with compassion. "The last thing I want is to hurt you."

I shake my head. "Don't worry yourself about that.

We're two grown adults."

In a bold move, she reaches over to take my hand. "I'd hate to risk ruining what we have."

"But I want to explore a more intimate relationship with you," I tell her, squeezing her hand. "I understand your hesitancy. However, if that is the only reason, why don't we head over to the dungeon after we're done here and I'll test it out."

She looks at me questioningly. "How?"

"I'll share you with another Dom and see how I feel about it."

"Are you sure you're ready for that?"

"How can I know unless I put myself in the situation? The real question here is are you willing to try?"

"Are you kidding? The idea of scening with two Doms makes me all tingly inside."

"Good." I look down at my plate. "I think I'm done here. How about you?"

She answers with a confident, "Yes."

After getting the attention of our waiter, I ask him to box up our meals.

I watch in satisfaction as she squirms in her seat under my lustful gaze. I imagine she's already wet just thinking about the evening ahead.

"I know exactly who I want to ask," I tell her as we head out. Before she can ask who, I put my finger to her lips.

"No questions, darlin'."

It makes our drive to the dungeon even more stimulating as I look at my sweet, innocent date, in her bright yellow dress, knowing she is about to have the night of her life.

I can feel the weight of everyone's gaze as the two of us enter the dungeon. Then the whispering starts…

People don't know what to make of us coming to the dungeon in our street clothes after our vanilla date.

"Cattleman!" Durov calls to me from beside the St. Andrew's cross.

I was hoping he would be here, even though Thane wasn't here because he had to finish a research paper.

After entering the dungeon, it's expected that you adhere to protocol, so I command glee to kneel where she is, head bowed, and command her to wait.

Leaving her there, I walk over to the other side of the dungeon to speak with the Russian. I see his brow is covered in sweat as he finishes wiping down the St. Andrew's cross. "Just finished with a session?"

He swipes the back if his hand against his brow. "*Da.* A satisfying one, at that."

Durov nods to where glee is kneeling. "I see glee is with you tonight." He leans in close and whispers, "Did she respond positively to your proposal?"

"Yes, but I will be testing our perimeters tonight."

"How so?"

"I know you just finished, but would you consider scening with the two of us?"

He raises an eyebrow. "A threesome? Two Doms and one sub?"

"Yes."

He scans the dungeon, smirking as he looks at the other Doms. "That is highly unusual."

"It may be, but I think the challenge of it would help me to determine whether I can give glee what she needs."

I figure if I am going to have any feelings of jealousy, watching Durov pleasure her while I pleasure her would certainly rile it up.

I know how fond she is of the Russian…

Durov says nothing as he puts the cleaning supplies away. "You never cease to surprise me, cattleman." He glances at glee. "Two Doms scening with one woman will raise eyebrows and even invite possible ridicule to us both."

I was afraid he would turn me down because of that, and am surprised when he adds, "But I enjoy stirring the pot."

"So, you'll do it then?"

He flexes his throwing arm. "I'm not sure I have another session in me so soon."

"There's no need to use the 'nines. I was thinking more along the lines of a little breath play while she pleasures you with her mouth."

Durov smiles, his gaze returning to glee kneeling on the floor. "*Da*, that would do."

"I'm going to surprise her with my choice of Dom by blindfolding her."

His lips curl into a wicked grin. "Excellent."

I pick up a blindfold before walking back over to her. "Glee."

She immediately looks up. Gone is the shy girl I took out to dinner. In her place is the confident sub I've come to know.

"Yes, Master."

"Stand and turn away from me."

Glee rises to her feet and turns, holding her breath as I place the blindfold over her eyes and secure it tightly.

"Strip."

Glee bites her bottom lip as she shimmies out of her yellow dress. She looks so innocent, standing there in her little white panties and bra. Those quickly fall to the floor, as well.

"Take my hand," I tell her. Rather than retreat to a private room, which would only incite speculation, I decide to perform our scene in the open. I guide her to the spanking bench.

After helping her onto it, I give her tempting ass a hard smack and grin as the sound of her satisfied squeal fills the dungeon.

"Glee, tonight you will pleasure two of us."

"Yes, Master," she answers breathlessly.

I move behind her, taking my time as I rid myself of my clothes. My shaft is already hard just looking at her glistening pussy and I reach down to play with her clit.

Pressing my rigid cock against her, I ask, "Would you like to know who your other Master is tonight?"

"Yes…"

Durov moves up to her, his hard dick ready to penetrate those pretty lips.

I tease her pussy with the head of my shaft and command, "Open your mouth."

Glee dutifully parts her lips, moaning softly as she waits.

Taking a fistful of her hair, Durov slowly guides his cock into her mouth. "Deeper," he growls in his thick Russian accent as he forces it down her throat.

Glee moans in pleasure as soon as she hears his voice, and she unconsciously arches her back in reaction to his presence.

I stay still, observing them both while I watch glee deep throat him. Even though it's apparent they're both thoroughly enjoying themselves, I feel no hint of jealousy—yet. And I'm encouraged by that.

Taking her sexy little ass in both hands, I press my cock against her opening and groan in satisfaction as it slips inside her wet pussy millimeter by sensual millimeter. She moans loudly from the challenge the girth of my cock provides.

That's when Durov reaches around to pinch her nipples. She squirms against me, obviously loving the dual attention. The Russian chuckles sadistically as he continues to play with her nipples, making her squirm even more.

I spank her ass several times and demand she take all of me.

Glee pulls her mouth away from Durov's cock long enough to answer, "Yes, Master. Fuck me with that huge cock of yours."

Damn, that girl turns me on…

"You have permission to come, glee—multiple times."

I give a hard thrust and glee moans around Durov's

shaft. I love the power I feel and begin pounding into her.

Soon, I hear glee's muffled screams as her tight pussy takes all of my substantial cock. I look at Rytsar, who pulls out of her mouth and leans down to whisper something to her.

She nods even as her head bounces with every stroke of my cock.

Taking her head in both hands, Durov gazes down at her with a ravenous look as he begins fucking her mouth in rhythm with my strokes. Then he suddenly stops, holding her head still as I continue to thrust into her.

She stiffens for a moment before her body relaxes, goosebumps covering her skin.

Pulling his shaft out, glee takes a deep breath of air. When she's ready for more, she opens her mouth wide for him.

Durov forces his cock down her throat, claiming it. When he stops again with his shaft deep in her throat, glee completely relaxes.

I stop thrusting and feel her pussy tightening rhythmically as she's gripped by an intense orgasm. The sound of her pleasure is muffled by the Russian's cock, and it almost sends me over the edge.

I ramp back up, following Durov's lead as we fuck glee from both ends. When he makes a low, guttural cry, climaxing into her throat, I close my eyes.

Savoring the wet constriction of her pussy, I pump my seed into her.

Glee's body shudders with one final orgasm, milking my spent cock. I groan in satisfaction as I slowly pull out and watch my come spill from her thoroughly fucked pussy.

Rytsar pulls away, leaving glee gasping for breath, but there's no denying the smile playing on those sexy lips. Her small frame trembles afterward, her skin drenched in sweat.

I undo her blindfold and kiss glee's glistening forehead. She looks up at me with a look of pure adoration, too weak from the intense orgasms to speak.

I glance over at Durov and nod. Not only do I feel satisfied with the scene we've just played out, but now I have no doubt I can handle sharing glee with other Doms.

Lifting glee into my arms, I cradle her against my chest.

Looking at her, I wonder again if she might be the one.

No Escape

I've been struggling for days with an equation in Applied Calculus, the class Thane insisted I take because of that little bet we had our freshman year. This problem is a special test the professor handed out during the first class—and it's ridiculously hard.

I'm frustrated to the point that I finally decide to confront Thane about the damn math problem. I find him in the library, and I huff loudly as I sit down beside him.

He slowly looks up from his textbook and smirks. "What's wrong?"

I slap the paper containing all my scribbles on the table. "There's no possible way to solve this equation."

He picks up my paper and studies it, nodding his head several times. Looking up, he slides it back over to me. "You've made good headway."

"That doesn't help me!"

Thane smiles. "Personally, I find solving a compli-cated equation is similar to figuring out how to please a woman."

"How so?"

"When I finally solve it, it's as if I'm experiencing a mental orgasm."

"But that still doesn't help me solve it, buddy."

Thane chuckles as he starts gathering his books and stuffing them into his backpack. "I wrote down a hint the professor gave out which finally helped me solve it. Let me get that for you."

His eyes shine with excitement as he slings his backpack on to his shoulder. "She's brilliant, the way she teaches this class. By doling out seemingly random bits of information during each lecture, she prepares you for situations you'll come across in business. The fact is, life doesn't hand you simple equations that can be easily solved."

I growl under my breath. At the moment, I'm having trouble appreciating the professor's brilliance.

He slaps me on the back as we exit the library. "To tell you the truth, I'm impressed with the direction you're taking with the equation. You're farther along than I was at that point."

"Really? Good to know," I answer, my frustration lessening after Thane's rare compliment.

As we head back to the dorm, a girl in a pink bikini walks past. I naturally turn my head to admire her fine, curvy ass accentuated by the bright pink thong.

I love the craziness that is college life in LA.

Thane murmurs angrily under his breath, "Fuck…"

I glance at him, wondering what his problem is, surprised to see him frowning. Following the direction of his focus, I notice a crowd forming around our dorm building.

"What the hell?" I exclaim.

Thane doesn't answer, lowering his head as he walks straight toward the mob. As we draw nearer, I'm shocked to see it's a group of reporters. As soon as they spot Thane, they start shouting like a flock of parrots.

"Mr. Davis, do you have a statement in regard to your mother's accusations against you?"

"Is it true you tried to have her killed?"

"Did you really send your own mother to jail?"

"Thane, look over here…"

I stick by his side as he plows through them like a bull in a china shop. The reporters push against me, trying to get closer to my friend, but I won't let them. It isn't until we make it to the entrance of the building and shut the doors forcibly behind us that we finally find ourselves alone.

"What the fuck was that?" I cry.

Thane says nothing.

A kid from our dorm walks up to Thane, demanding, "Is what they say true?"

Instead of replying, Thane turns abruptly and heads straight for the stairs.

I immediately follow behind him, the empty stairwell echoing with our hurried footsteps.

Thane takes the stairs two at a time all the way up to the third floor. In the hallway, several more guys stop us wanting to know what's going on.

I push them out of the way before unlocking the door to our room so Thane can disappear inside.

"Holy shit…" I mutter once we're safe inside.

Thane doesn't even look at me as he grabs his earphones and retreats to his bed.

I stand there stunned, shocked by the lingering feeling of defilement left by the throng of reporters. I can't imagine what Thane must be feeling, knowing all those vultures are here for him.

Someone starts banging on the door and I yell, "Knock it off before I open that door and punch you in the face."

Once they leave, I sit down on my bed and stare at Thane, feeling only sympathy for the guy.

He lays there, eyes closed, music cranked up, trying to come to grips with what's happening outside.

It felt so violent and invasive…

The poor guy still isn't free of his insane mother, even after everything we did to get her into the hands of the authorities. Understanding that Thane needs space to wrap his head around this new sneak attack, I start back on that problem, determined to figure it out on my own.

After midnight, I finally call it quits and glance over at him. Thane hasn't changed position, but the expression on his face unnerves me. It looks as if he's given up.

Thane can't quit now—I won't let him.

I get up and give Thane a nudge, but he keeps his eyes closed, only shaking his head.

Respecting his need for more time, I turn off the lights and slip into bed, trusting he will see things in a different light by morning.

Unfortunately, I'm wrong.

Thane wakes me up just as the sun is rising. It's obvious by his bloodshot eyes that he hasn't gotten a wink of sleep. With a sober expression, he announces, "I'm dropping out."

I bolt out of bed. "Like hell you are!"

"This is only the beginning of the harassment. The Beast won't let up until I'm kicked out of here. You've already had a taste of how tenacious she is." He shakes his head. "I thought I'd beaten her at her own game, but all I did was change the location of her attack."

Grabbing Thane by the shoulders, I shake him roughly. "I'm not going to let you quit. Do you hear me?"

He snarls at me, gesturing outside. "We can't fight this. I've tried. Once the press gets involved, there's no escape."

"You're wrong," I insist.

Thane turns his anger on me. "You have no idea what I've been through! I fought tooth and nail when the press attacked me as a child—a fucking child, for God's sake—and I still came out the loser."

"But you were alone." Folding my arms across my chest, I tell him, "You are not alone anymore."

"It's not enough. She'll break you, too."

My lips curl into a smile. "I'd like to see her try."

Thane won't budge. "This isn't your battle, Anderson. I guarantee your name will be dragged through the mud. Even if you don't care, your family doesn't deserve the humiliation they'll be subjected to."

I snort. "My family can handle it. They've never been afraid of what others think."

"Damn it!" he growls, getting frustrated with me.

"Think about your sisters. As their brother, it's your duty to protect them."

"You don't understand, buddy. Our town is a tight-knit group. They know who we are, so lies don't hold power over us."

Thane stands back for a moment, muttering to himself, "Damn...I wish I knew that kind of family loyalty."

"So, there's no need for you to waste your energy worrying about me or my family. What you *need* to do is to come up with a plan to combat her newest attack."

He sighs heavily. "It's pointless. These attacks will never end. It's better for everyone if I disappear before it gets any worse."

I put an arm around him. "You really want to give the Beast that satisfaction?"

"No…"

"Well, lucky for you, you don't have to." I slap my thigh. "'Cause I'm feeling the same buzz I had when I mounted Crusher. But this time, I'm staying on the bull till the buzzer sounds and the Beast is conquered."

Thane stares at me thoughtfully before stating, "I never appreciated how much your risk-taking behavior shapes your choices. Was there a catalyst that got you started down that path?"

Paige's face instantly comes to mind.

It's almost as if Thane can read the pain behind my silence, because he immediately replies, "No need to answer that."

The kid is spooky that way—his uncanny ability to read people so easily.

"If we're going to ditch those reporters, we'd better

get you out of here now while it's still early," I tell him.

Thane nods and starts throwing his textbooks into his backpack, but then he stops and looks at me.

"Thank you, Brad."

I'm taken aback and joke, "Wow, calling me by my first name…what's the occasion?"

"I think you're crazy for sticking by me."

"Well, I live for a good challenge, and your beast of a mother is the ultimate."

Thane's chuckle is tainted with sarcasm as he finishes gathering his supplies. He slings his backpack over his shoulder and walks over to me.

Laying a hand on my shoulder, he says somberly, "You can bail when you start having second thoughts."

I burst out laughing. "Are you kidding? Once I have the rope in my grip and my knees clenched around the bull, there's nothing stopping me from finishing the ride."

Thane slips out the back of the building while I head through the front. I'm shocked to see one young report-er perk up as soon as I open the door. When he sees me, however, he can't hide his frown when he asks, "Hey, do you know Thane Davis?"

I shake my head as I turn and go in the opposite di-rection.

He starts following me. "Would you be willing to go on record? I don't need specifics, just your general impressions of the guy."

I walk a little faster, growling behind me, "Why don't you get a real job instead of harassing college students?"

"Asshole…" he mutters, heading back to the entrance of the dorm.

I have to hand it to Thane. I gave him no end of shit for keeping to himself like a hermit his freshman year, but now I understand the reason behind it.

The most reporters are going to get from his fellow classmates is that he's often seen at the library and pretty much keeps to himself.

No one on campus. other than Durov, Clark, and I, know about his alternative lifestyle, or that he often frequents the dungeon.

Thankfully, Thane can trust everyone at the dungeon because silence in that small BDSM community is a given.

I suspect the reporters are going to have a difficult time getting information on him, and they'll be forced to move on after a few days.

I walk a little faster to catch up with Thane as he heads into the small coffee shop just off campus.

"You already had one of those reporters waiting for you," I tell him as I settle down in the seat beside him.

"Why am I not surprised?" he growls.

"So, what's the plan?" I ask him, after ordering two cinnamon rolls.

"I need to stay hidden, but I still have to attend all my classes. To graduate early I can't let even one class slip."

"It's important you stick to that plan, that's why I'm

determined to help you."

The waitress hands me two dishes with large cinnamon rolls. I slide one over to Thane.

He stares at it, stating, "I'd prefer to skip breakfast. Besides, Durov should be here any second."

"You need sustenance after the kind of night you've had," I insist.

"I'd rather not," he tells me, still staring at the ooey gooey bun of perfection.

"Live a little, buddy." I take a bite of my cinnamon roll and groan in pleasure as the warm bread melts in my mouth and the sweet cinnamon plays on my tongue. "Nothing tastes better in the morning. Trust me."

He gives me a side glance, but grins slightly. "I can think of one thing I'd rather taste."

Even in the face of adversity, Thane still has a dirty mind.

I like that.

I watch with satisfaction as he finally takes that first bite. Thane knows I'm watching and chews it without any expression on his face, but there's no hiding how good it is, and he eventually smiles.

"Do I know my way around food or what?" I boast. "I will never steer you wrong."

Durov bursts into the café and immediately waltzes over to us. "Okay, who needs to get roughed up?"

"Hold your horses," I tell him. "You can't go disturbing the cinnamon roll experience." I hold up my hand and instruct our waitress to get us another one.

Durov sits down opposite Thane, exuding malevolence.

The guy could be dangerous if left to his own devices…

Before he has a chance to pump Thane for more information, the lovely waitress sets a cinnamon roll in front of him.

"We need to talk—" he insists, pushing it away.

"Eh, eh…no talking." I push the plate back and hand him a fork before taking another bite of my roll.

With a huff, Durov stabs at the cinnamon roll. He takes a bite and looks surprised, flashing me a rare grin. "This is similar to *plushka*. My mother makes the best."

"I would like to see a showdown between your mama and mine," I tell him, certain my mother would win.

"No offense, cattleman, but my *mamulya* would decimate your sweet mother in the kitchen."

I laugh good-heartedly. "I doubt that very much."

"How about a bet, then?" he states. "I'll pay for your mother to fly to Russia so you can put your claim to the test."

I don't know if he's joking, but I immediately take him up on it. "Anytime, anywhere. I'm confident my mama will outcook yours."

"Huh," he snorts, taking another bite of his roll.

I notice Thane silently watching our exchange and suddenly realize it must be hard for him to hear us go on and on about our mothers when his is such a royal bitch.

"Any ideas on how to thwart the reporters?" I ask him, wanting to change the subject.

Thane holds up his hand while he finishes chewing. "Before I say anything more, I want to give Samantha a chance to get here."

I instantly see Durov perk up. "What? She's coming?"

"Yes. I felt it was necessary, considering the Beast contacted the three of you personally last time. I'm afraid that however this plays out, you may all suffer because of her."

Durov quickly finishes his cinnamon roll, looking at his hands in irritation. "Unlike my mother's *plushka,* this is a sticky mess."

"It makes eating it all the more fun," I tell him, licking my fingers with relish.

He huffs as he stands up and excuses himself to go wash his hands.

Once he's out of earshot, I mutter to Thane, "I never thought the Russian would be susceptible to the wiles of a woman. It's kind of cute."

He chuckles in agreement. "I do find it amusing."

Samantha walks through the door, sounding breathless, and unknowingly takes Durov's seat. "I got here as soon as I could."

"I appreciate it," Thane tells her. "But I'd prefer it if we were meeting under better circumstances—"

Durov clears his throat behind Samantha and says in his thick Russian accent, "You have taken my seat."

She glances up, ready to challenge him. Then—for no apparent reason—she suddenly becomes mute when their eyes meet.

Durov holds out his hand to her. Without a moment's hesitation, she takes it and he directs her to the chair beside him, giving her hand a lingering kiss before letting go.

Samantha blushes as she sits down.

Although Thane is watching them intently, he lets their unusual exchange pass without comment.

"Now that you are all here, I want to explain what happened last night." He glances over at me. "As I mentioned on the phone, Anderson and I were accosted by a mob of reporters outside the dorm."

"I'd be happy to smash each and every one of their faces, comrade," Durov asserts, grinding his fist into his palm.

"As much as I might enjoy it, that would definitely not help the situation," Thane says with a snort.

He continues, his voice growing angrier each word. "Apparently, my mother is accusing me of planning to kill her for her money and told the reporters that when she discovered my plan, I hid my guilt by claiming she was crazy and getting her locked up."

"Nobody is going to believe her," Samantha scoffs.

Thane states somberly, "The Beast already has several lawyers offering to represent her."

"It means nothing," Durov assures him.

Thane looks at all of us. "Anderson offered to help combat this latest attack, but here's the thing. I can guarantee you that if I stay here, it will directly impact each of you. She won't hesitate to hurt you if it will hurt me."

I'm heartened when both Durov and Samantha dismiss his misgivings and immediately offer their support, too.

Thane holds up his hand to stop them. "While I deeply appreciate your offer, it's not only the three of you who would be at risk. I'm concerned about the potential impact on glee and the dungeon itself. *Anything* associated with me is at risk…"

He pauses for a moment, and I can tell by the way his voice catches that what he is about to say is difficult for him. "…which is why it would be best if I leave now."

When I start to protest, Thane interrupts me. "I knew last year that I was a taking a risk by coming to this campus. I never intended to make friends. It was an error on my part, because I know how dangerous my mother is, and…I'm sorry."

"We're not cowards," Durov states emphatically.

"I know that," Thane says with restrained calm. "However, you have no idea what the press will dig up. You could lose your student visa and get sent home. It's not worth that risk."

"So? I finish my studies in Russia," Durov answers with a shrug.

Seeing he's making no headway with Durov, Thane turns to Samantha. "We both know that if my mother ever catches wind of our private lessons or your association with glee, she has the potential of not only trashing your reputation, but dividing your family. Trust me, it's not worth chancing your future."

Samantha purses her lips and glances at Durov briefly before answering. "Maybe the time has come for me to own who I am."

Thane sits back in his chair, clearly frustrated. "I don't seem to be getting through to any of you. This isn't a game."

Knowing what needs to happen, I take the reins. "Look, you've worked too damn hard to get to this point. No way are we letting you quit when we're all willing to fight for you."

Instead of seeing reason, Thane growls. "You have no idea how bad it will get."

I chuckle. "Hey, if it gets too rough, we'll all move to Durov's beach house."

Durov nods his approval.

But Thane vehemently opposes the idea. "I guarantee that mob of reporters will descend on us there. It would jeopardize your residence and the neighbors around you."

Durov leans forward. "You act as if I am unfamiliar with this type of thing."

Thane seems taken aback.

"What you fail to realize is that I have a network of people who can help in this situation." He smiles wickedly, raising an eyebrow. "You'd be surprised what I can make happen."

Thane interlocks his fingers as he contemplates Durov's offer.

Durov continues, "My people can get you wherever you need to go. The reporters will find it nearly impossible to harass you with my men there."

Thane nods. It looks like Durov is winning him over until Durov leans in close and adds in an ominous tone, "Understand, I have no problem getting my hands dirty—should the need arise."

Thane's defenses suddenly return. "That is one thing you *cannot* do."

"Fine," the Russian replies nonchalantly, smiling in my direction and shrugging to let me know he tried. "We're willing to play by your rules, comrade…just as long as you stay."

Thane lets out a long sigh, still not convinced. So, I put my hand in the center of the table, stating in no uncertain terms, "I'm all in."

Rytsar immediately covers mine and agrees, "All in."

Samantha places her hand on top, echoing Durov. "All in."

Thane finally concedes, putting his hand over Samantha's. "Then I guess I'm staying." However, his eyes dart to each of us in concern. "None of you deserves this complication in your lives."

Looking him dead in the eye, I tell him, "Neither do you, buddy."

Breaking Point

Later that afternoon, I head back to the dorm and decide to have a little fun with the horde of reporters milling around the building.

"Run, Thane, run!" I cry, pointing to some random guy who vaguely resembles my roommate.

The gaggle of reporters turn as one and start running toward him. The kid freezes in his tracks for a second before bolting in the opposite direction.

I chuckle to myself as I walk into the building.

"Mr. Anderson? Can I have a moment of your time?"

I look at the one lone reporter smart enough not to follow the group. I shake my head. "I don't have time for people like you."

"Please, I—"

I turn away and shut the door on him with a sense of righteousness.

Reporters are the scum of the earth…

I have to say I'm impressed with how quickly Durov

is able to assemble a party of men to stick by Thane's side. My friend now has a human barrier between him and all the journalists, so he can attend his classes and then return to the dorm untouched, although his new entourage still have to push through them.

Unfortunately, that isn't stopping the speculations about Thane from growing.

"Anderson!" one of my friends calls out as I wait for the elevator.

"What's up, James?"

I can tell the guy is riled up as he approaches me. "Why the hell are you still rooming with that criminal?"

"You have no idea what you're talking about," I answer dismissively, turning my back on him.

He puts his hand on my shoulder and jerks me around to face him. "You'd better sleep with one eye open, because that freaky fucker killed his father and is gunning for his mother now. The kid is seriously unbalanced."

My hand automatically forms into a fist, but I fight the urge to sock him in the face. "Are you really stupid enough to believe any of that crap?"

He sets his jaw. "You're actually defending the freak?" He shakes his head, snarling under his breath, "Something's not quite right between you two…"

I get up in his face. "Not another word, jackass."

"Oh, shit!" He backs away from me with a look of revulsion. "I bet the two of you are banging each other. I've always wondered why you two sneak off together at night."

I push him away as the elevator doors open, but he

follows me inside and socks me in the gut, bellowing, "You're a fucking faggot!"

After the doors close, I start whaling on him, feeling no compunction about letting loose. My pop always taught me that you never start a fight, but you sure as hell finish one.

By the time the elevator opens on the third floor, I have the asshole subdued in a lump on the floor. Wiping my bleeding lip, I look down and tell him, "Go fuck yourself, James."

I head to my room and clean my face up, thinking nothing of it. I trust I've taught any other assholes who might be questioning my roommate's integrity to think twice.

Thane doesn't arrive until after dark. As soon as he sees my busted lip, he gets overly upset.

"Fuck! It's already started."

"Nothing happened, man. James just needed to be corrected. Trust me. He looks *way* worse than I do."

"Why would you fight with him in the first place? It's imperative you keep your head low."

"You weren't there. I didn't lift a damn finger until he threw the first punch."

"Why did he hit you in the first place?"

I tilt my head, cracking my neck to keep my composure, before I tell him, "He believes you're a killer and that…" I pause, unsure if I should tell him.

"That what?" Thane demands.

"That I swing from both branches."

He furrows his brow. "Why would he believe that?"

"The asshole thinks we're sneaking off at night to

bang each other."

Thane closes his eyes, muttering. "Of course, he does. Makes perfect sense."

"But don't give it another thought. I explained to him how it is—with my fist."

"Damn it! You're no different than Durov."

"Like hell I am! I didn't throw the first punch *or* the first insult."

The uneasy look Thane gives me sends chills down my spine. "I'm afraid for you, Anderson."

I laugh off his unwarranted concern. "Why? This isn't the first time I've been in a fist fight."

"You don't understand how serious this is." He sighs, adding sadly, "But, you soon will."

"Hey, there's no reason to sweat this, buddy. I've ridden a champion bull, remember? Nothing can faze me."

There's a haunted look in Thane's eyes when he tells me, "Nothing compares to the cruelty of people."

Another chill shoots down my spine, but I immediately laugh it off.

The next day, I'm pulled out of my calculus class and told to report directly to the dean's office.

I'm still clueless as to how bad things are until I enter the room. There I'm confronted by the college hierarchy and all three men wear serious expressions.

"Sit down," Dean Abernathy orders.

I look at him questioningly, shaking my head in disbelief. "What's this all about?"

"Sit," he barks again.

I do what he says, but I'm confused by the harsh treatment.

"Were you involved in an altercation yesterday involving another student?"

"Yes."

"Are you aware that assault is grounds for dismissal?"

"But I didn't start it."

"We have a witness that says otherwise."

"That's bullshit! James attacked *me*. First, the asshole accused me of being gay, then he started punching me in the elevator and calling me a faggot."

The dean slowly laces his fingers together, looking extremely annoyed. "You will address me *properly*, Mr. Anderson, and refrain from using foul language in this office."

I sweep my hair back. "Look, I'm sorry, Dean Abernathy." I glance at the other two men. "I apologize to all of you for my inappropriate language, but James is flat-out lying."

The man on the right speaks first. "It's come to our attention that you and Mr. Davis may be involved in illegal activities."

I throw my head back and laugh. "You can't be serious."

He gives me a stern glare. "I assure you, we are."

Dean Abernathy asks, "Can you explain where the two of you go at night when you leave the campus?"

Fuck…I can't say a word about the dungeon.

Thinking fast on my feet, I answer, "What we do off campus is of no consequence to you or this college."

The second man huffs, turning to the other two. "I find it interesting that he's *not* answering a simple question."

I direct my attention toward Dean Abernathy. "I've done nothing wrong, sir."

He picks up a file with my name on it and frowns. "I've looked into your records, and I see you were charged with vandalism as a minor."

I laugh, remembering that epic prank in high school. "It was a practical joke. Nothing criminal about it."

"What it shows is a propensity toward unlawful acts or, at the very least, a serious lack of sound judgement."

I close my eyes, trying to rein in my anger. "Last night I was attacked by James McDougal. *He* harassed me and then threw the first punch. All I was trying to do was defend myself."

"That's not what he told us."

Dean Abernathy clears his throat, handing me a photo. "This picture was taken earlier this morning."

I hide my smile as I stare down at James' face. Damn…he looks a lot worse than I do.

Serves the fucker right.

Rubbing my split lip, I tell the dean, "Sir, my father raised me right. I never instigate a fight, and I never throw the first punch. But, if someone attacks me, I'm damn well going to teach them not to do it again."

"Violence is not acceptable. Those outlaw tactics may work in rural Colorado, but they're not tolerated here."

The chill I felt last night returns when I realize they might kick me out. "What can I do to convince you I'm not the bad guy here?"

The man on the right looks at me with a condescending smile. "Explain to us where you go with Mr. Davis at night. Are you selling illegal drugs?"

"Of course not!"

"What then?"

There's no way out of this without exposing the dungeon. I sigh, the feeling of defeat washing over me. "I can't say, sir."

"Then we have no other choice than to put you on probation for the assault while we decide your fate at this institution."

"What about James?"

"His future is no concern of yours," Dean Abernathy states, closing the subject for discussion.

Even though this is total bullshit, I can't afford to lose class time, and I am not above begging. "Please, don't put me on probation. I've been working hard this year—just ask my professors. You can't let that idiot's lies ruin everything I'm working for. Please, Dean Abernathy."

"Not another word, young man, unless you want me to expel you right now."

Knowing my back's up against the wall, I stand up and nod to them. Before I open the door to leave, however, I turn around to tell them, "I trust justice will prevail."

Their silence is my only answer, so I force myself to

swallow down my anger as I quietly shut the door behind me.

I can't believe how quickly things have gotten out of control. Thane wasn't kidding about how bad things would get.

On my way back to my room, several reporters confront me, trying to pump me for information.

"Get the fuck away from me," I yell at them. "All of you!"

"Mr. Anderson, if you would just let Mr. Davis—"

I see it's that persistent reporter I had to shut the door on yesterday. "Don't even, man…" I warn him. "I am so *not* in the mood."

"But—"

I growl ominously as I escape into the building, cutting him off before he can say anything else to piss me off.

Fuck, it hasn't even been forty-eight hours yet and I'm already going crazy. I can't even imagine the hell Thane went through when he was younger.

I take the stairs, wanting to avoid people as I head up to my room. Once I lock the door, I turn around and let out a loud roar of frustration.

"Fuck! Fuck! Fuck!"

I can't believe James McDougal, who had his ass handed to him after his little stunt last night, had the nerve to go to the dean and blame *me* for it.

I start pacing, wondering what the hell my parents are going to think when I tell them I'm on probation with the possibility of expulsion.

I stop in my tracks when I hear a clamber outside,

before someone unlocks the door. When it swings opens, I see Durov's hired men surrounding Thane. He scoots inside, growling as he shuts the door behind him, "This is getting fucking ridiculous!"

"What's got you all riled up?" I ask, surprised to see him as upset as I am.

"I've been told I'm no longer welcome at the dungeon because they can't afford the risk of exposure."

"Damn it! But if that's the case, I won't go, either."

"You're not the problem. As long as you steer clear of me, you're free to go."

"Not after today," I answer, attempting to sound light, even though I can't hide the strain in my voice.

"Why? What happened to you?" Thane asks, looking concerned.

"I've been put on probation. Dean Abernathy is considering expelling me from the school."

"What the hell for?"

I explain what happened, shaking my head afterward. "It's a fucked-up world when I'm the one in trouble, not fucking James McDougal."

"Unfortunately, I can't protect you from this shitstorm."

"I don't expect you to."

Thane puts his hand on my shoulder. "But you shouldn't put your college career in jeopardy defending me."

"I've done nothing wrong."

Thane looks at me gravely. "Being right isn't always enough." He goes to the window and gazes down at the reporters. "This isn't worth it, Anderson."

I see that determined look in his eye when he heads toward the door and know he's up to no good. But, before I can stop him, Thane leaves the room.

The guy's so fast, he's already down the stairs before I can catch up. "Whatever you're going to do, don't do it."

Thane ignores me and heads outside, so I follow right behind him.

He presence creates pure chaos.

Durov's men instantly surround Thane, but the mob of reporters pushes against them, trying to get to him.

The air is filled with the constant click of cameras and the sound of reporters yelling questions at Thane.

I notice that obnoxious reporter from before weaseling his way toward my buddy, so I head him off, grabbing his shirt.

"Fuck you all!" Thane yells above the din. "What will it take to get you to leave me the hell alone?"

The reporters start screaming questions, holding their microphones out, hoping to record his breakdown.

"Mr. Anderson!" the little weasel I've got in my grasp shouts. "Don't let your friend say another word. My name is Harold Thompson. I'm here because I want to represent Mr. Davis as his lawyer."

I let the guy go, looking at him in surprise—all this time, he just wanted to help.

"Sorry about that, man," I apologize as I start pushing him toward Thane.

"Thane, buddy! You need to talk to this guy *now*!" I yell over the clamor of reporters.

Thane looks over at me and nods at the bodyguards,

who part enough to let Thompson through their ring of protection. I watch as the guy whispers something in Thane's ear.

Afterward, Thane looks at me, gesturing that I should follow him.

Thompson leads us to his car with the mob of reporters milling around us every step of the way. It would be funny if it weren't so incredibly annoying.

Thankfully, Durov's men are able to keep the reporters at bay while we can get into the vehicle. Once the three of us are inside, Thane's bodyguards part the crowd of reporters so Thompson can take off.

I breathe a sigh of relief, glad to be free of that feeding frenzy.

Thane turns to Thompson, "Thank you. I hit my breaking point."

"I could tell," he says somberly.

I clap Thompson on the shoulder from the backseat. "Damn, and all this time I thought you were one of them. Sorry about that."

Glancing at Thane, Thompson says, "It's been impossible for me to get near you. You have quite the devoted team protecting you."

Thane looks at me and nods. "I do."

Turning back to Thompson, Thane asks, "What is it you want?"

"I would like to represent you. There's no reason you should have to put up with this harassment."

"I have no money to pay you," Thane states bluntly.

"I plan to work pro bono."

Thane stares at him suspiciously. "Why would you

do that?"

"Alonzo was a remarkable talent. My parents were big fans of your father's music and I grew up listening to his violin as a child. Our entire family was devastated when your father passed away unexpectedly."

I notice Thane flinch, but he doesn't lose his composure. "It's true. My father died too young."

Thompson glances at Thane, stating somberly. "It was horrifying how the media turned against him following the tragic circumstances of his death. It was unconscionable." He gives Thane a look of compassion. "While there was nothing I could do to help back then, when I heard about this latest attack on you, I felt compelled to offer my services. I may be fresh out of law school, Mr. Davis, but I promise you that my drive makes up for my lack of experience."

Thane smiles appreciatively. "There's a lot to be said for a man with initiative."

"Then you'll let me represent you?"

Thane looks at me. "What about my friend, Anderson? He's been set up and is facing expulsion because of me."

Thompson glances in the review mirror and asks me, "What happened?"

I explain the altercation with McDougal, and the subsequent fallout.

"Don't concern yourself with their threat of expulsion. I'm certain the surveillance cameras will clearly define who was at fault and what witnesses, if any, were present. It sounds like the administration is uncomfortable with the publicity this is bringing to the college and is quietly trying to eliminate the issue without regard to who gets burned in the process."

"So, you'd be willing to take me on, too?" I ask Thompson hopefully.

"Your threat of expulsion is a direct result of your involvement with Mr. Davis. Of course, I'll help."

"There is something I should make you aware of before you make a commitment to either of us," Thane tells him.

"What?"

Thane glances at me. "Are you okay with me telling him?"

I know he's talking about our involvement with the dungeon. Although we made a vow not to tell others about its existence, it would be unwise to keep it from the man who plans to defend us. Besides, I feel no shame about my involvement with the dungeon. "If you trust him with the knowledge, then I agree it's necessary."

Thane nods and turns toward him. "Thompson, are you familiar with BDSM?"

He immediately answers, "In concept, yes."

"You should know that both Anderson and I are part of a secret group who practice BDSM. We cannot afford to have our group exposed. The only reason I mention it is that McDougal has noticed us leaving the dorm together at night on multiple occasions. Our whereabouts were brought into question during Anderson's meeting with the dean. Whatever the consequences are, we won't out the people in our group."

Thompson nods, keeping silent as he mulls over the

information.

Thane adds, "If you do not feel you can represent us, I understand."

"I'll think you're a coward but, yeah, I'll understand, too," I tell the guy.

Thompson flashes a smile. "I like the honesty, Mr. Anderson."

"What can I say? I was raised to be upfront."

"An admirable trait, so let me be equally upfront. As far as your nightly excursions are concerned, they have nothing to do with the incident involving Mr. McDougal. I see no legal reason it should be addressed. It won't be a problem."

"But you'll keep the existence of the dungeon to yourself?" I prod.

He looks insulted. "I'm a professional, Mr. Anderson. Everything you share in confidence stays between us."

Thane rests his hand on Thompson's shoulder. "Anderson feels a responsibility to our friends at the dungeon. No offense was meant."

Thompson narrows his eyes, staring at me in the reflection of the rearview mirror. "I don't like my integrity being called into question, but if you need assurance, hand me a dollar."

I have no idea what the guy is up to, and chuckle as I fish out a dollar bill and hand it over to him.

"Good," he says after taking it. "Now that I've been technically hired, I'm duty-bound to keep your case confidential."

"Oh, you're good." I laugh, my concerns now lifted.

"So, what do you need from us?" Thane asks him.

"I went to the liberty of having a contract drawn up stating that I'm acting as your legal counsel which you can sign."

Looking in the rearview mirror, he tells me, "As for you, once I get one drawn up, I'll go directly to the president of the college and let him know I am legally representing you in this matter."

"How soon can you do that?"

"Early tomorrow."

"Damn, you're quick. That would be a huge relief for me."

"For both of us," Thane interjects. "I hate having my friends mistreated on my account."

"I can appreciate that," Thompson says as he pulls into a public parking lot overlooking the ocean.

He turns to Thane and asks, "Do you have any idea what the motivations are behind your mother's current accusations?"

Thane snorts angrily. "The Beast doesn't like to lose. My guess is she's trying to sway public opinion with the deluded belief that bringing my guilt into question will exonerate her. It doesn't hurt that it also feeds her perverse need to see me suffer."

"His mother is a monster," I tell the man.

Thompson nods. "I suspected that after her actions following Alonzo Davis' untimely death."

"My mother is exactly where she belongs," Thane states coldly.

"Agreed, Mr. Davis, and I will do everything in my power to legally protect you from her influence."

Thompson grabs his briefcase and gets out of the car. We follow him to an empty picnic table, where he asks Thane to sit beside him. Taking out the contract, he hands it to Thane and goes over each page, explaining the legal terminology so Thane understands exactly what he's signing.

I already like this Thompson guy.

After Thane signs it, the two stand up and shake hands.

"I cannot tell you how grateful I am for your help."

"It's my pleasure, Mr. Davis. I hope to have this issue resolved in a timely manner but, until then, you will need to keep that entourage around you, and neither of you can say a word to the press."

I chuckle. "Damn, ruin all my fun, why don't ya?"

But Thane frowns. "I hope this can be resolved quickly. The end of the semester is only a couple of weeks away and I do *not* want reporters invading my uncle's neighborhood trying to get to me."

I perk up. "Wait up, buddy. Did you forget you're celebrating Christmas with my family?"

He laughs it off. "I didn't think you were actually serious."

"You bet I was. My mom has been testing out new recipes for weeks now."

Thane groans. "Don't you understand? I dislike anything relating to Christmas. I'll only make your family miserable if I go."

For all of Thane's complaining, I notice Thompson seems pleased by the idea. "May I ask where your parents live, Mr. Anderson?"

"Greeley, Colorado."

Thompson turns to Thane. "The timing couldn't be better. You should go. The press can't harass you if they don't know where you are. In the meantime, I can get injunctions in place, so they won't be allowed on campus when you return."

Thane's look of relief is easy to read. "If you succeed, it would be a far better outcome than I ever thought possible."

"I *will* make it happen," he states.

I see the first real smile from Thane in weeks. "If you pull this off, Thompson, you will have a client for life."

Private Party

Knowing that Thane has been banned from the dungeon, Durov invites us to join him at a private play party being held in downtown LA.

"I can't let you two leave for Colorado without a proper sendoff," he tells us. "You need to be reminded of what you'll be missing while you're gone."

"A private party, huh?" I ask, thoroughly intrigued by the idea.

The Russian grins. "*Da.* I know several high-profile individuals who prefer the intimacy and exclusivity of a private party. It will be far less formal than the dungeon. However, the host has complete control on what is and is not allowed in their home."

"It's held at a home?" Thane asks, sounding surprised.

"If that's the case, then I'll need to bring Myrtle with me," I announce.

Durov nods. "*Da,* the ceilings are too low for a standard bullwhip."

The Russian then turns to Thane. "There will be several famous people in attendance, comrade."

"Having grown up with a world-renowned musician, that does nothing to excite me."

"I only mention it because it can mess with your head as a Dom when you are asked to dominate someone prominent in society."

"I appreciate what you're saying," Thane says, nodding. "So, what's your recommendation?"

Durov grins wickedly. "You treat them the same as you would any other sub. Many Dominants become intimidated by the elite here in LA and perform poorly because of it. But, for me, it adds an extra thrill. These people are used to having the power in social arenas. Once you strip that away, you'd be surprised how desperate they are to bend to your will."

"I'm grateful for the advice, my friend."

Durov turns to me. "That miniature bullwhip will be particularly popular at this gathering."

"Good to hear," I state, excited about the party. "Thanks again for the invite."

In an unusual moment of candidness, Durov confesses, "Your loyalty to my comrade is something I deeply respect. Far too many people in this world pledge friendship, but then abandon you the moment it becomes inconvenient."

"I have to admit when I first met you, Durov, I thought you were nothing but trouble. You are—so it turns out I was right."

Durov chuckles.

"However, I *am* grateful to call you my friend," I

add.

"Likewise, cattleman," he says, smacking me on the back.

The night of the event, I'm driven by one of Durov's men to a tower located in the heart of downtown LA.

I struggle to contain the nervous energy building in my bones. I can't believe I'm here—a cowboy from Colorado—about to unleash my bullwhip on some of the social elite of LA.

I'm told to wait in the car until Thane shows up in a separate vehicle. I've been instructed to wear a hoodie to cover my head and to bring a change of clothing as well as my tools for the evening in a gym bag.

When Thane shows up, every precaution is taken to ensure our identities remain hidden as we enter the building from a side entrance and are escorted to a private elevator. We look at each other in silence as we ride straight up to the penthouse.

The doors open to an impressive marble foyer where we are greeted by a young woman wearing only a collar and bejeweled nipple rings.

Bowing, she says, "Please follow me."

Holy shit, so this is how the upper echelon lives…

I watch her walk away, her shapely ass swaying seductively with every step, and then glance over at Thane.

I can't believe this is real.

She leads us to a set of double doors and tells us to

enter before bowing to both of us and leaving.

Thane pulls his hoodie down as he opens the doors and breaks out in a smile. "Fancy meeting you here."

I look from behind Thane to see Samantha standing in the room dressed in a red vinyl catsuit that emphasizes her long legs and hugs every curve of her body. With the red stilettos she's wearing, she's looking dangerous tonight.

She nods to both of us, saying in the confident voice of a Dominatrix, "Pleasure to see you both."

"Likewise," Thane answers.

I sweep back my hair, chuckling. "I have to say, Samantha. You clean up *real* nice."

She gives me a wicked half-smile that gets my blood pumping. I can totally appreciate why Durov is obsessed with her.

"Rytsar told me to get dressed and wait for him here. I assume you both should do the same."

Not one to be shy about my body, I immediately pull off the sweats, reaching into my gym bag for the black leather pants I bought for the occasion. I've decided to go kinky, but classy tonight. I complete my ensemble by slipping on a smoky gray t-shirt, a black cowboy hat and boots.

Pulling Myrtle out of my bag, I flick my wrist and she lets out a satisfying crack which echoes in the room.

Samantha jumps and blurts irritably, "You should give us a warning before you crack that damn thing."

"What would be the fun in that?" I ask, chuckling as I coil up my whip and secure it to my belt.

"Trust me. You get used to it," Thane tells her as he

buttons up his crisp white shirt before putting on a silk tie.

"Going with a suit again?" I comment, thinking both Samantha and I are killing it tonight with our new duds.

"A suit best expresses my style of dominance," he states.

I look Thane over, appreciating the truth of that statement. "Guess you're right."

Glancing at Samantha approvingly, I add, "I think we each hit the right chord in our choice of clothing."

Samantha pulls out a black crop from her bag and smiles seductively as she snaps it against her hand. "I can't wait to get started."

Thane looks like a proud parent as he stands there staring at her.

"You've truly come into your own, Samantha," he praises. "You're every bit the Domme I imagined you would be."

"I have you to thank for that. And, it wasn't just the lessons. Knowing that I might be outed by your beast of a mother has completely changed my perspective on things." She lifts her chin, adding with confidence, "There's no reason to feel shame for who I am and what I enjoy. I'm Samantha-fucking-Clark."

"Yes, you are," he agrees with admiration in his voice.

Samantha looks over at me. "And you can lick my stilettos if you don't like it."

The dominant vibe I'm picking up from her is alluring rather than abrasive. Seriously, I can't believe this sexy Domme standing before me is the same girl I met last year.

The doors open and I turn to see Durov standing in the doorway. He looks Thane and I over before his gaze lands on Samantha. "*Vy krasevaya...*" he murmurs huskily.

A blush rises to her cheeks.

Even though I don't know what he's just said, it is obvious by his tone that it's a high compliment.

In keeping with her Domme persona, Samantha give him a respectful nod. "Thank you."

He says nothing more but, based on the growing erection in his pants, he's noticeably affected by her beauty.

Forcing his gaze from her back to us, he breaks out in a grin. "Everyone is anxious to meet you three. First, you must socialize and partake in our host's hors d'oeuvres before you will be allowed to join in on the fun."

My cock starts aching as I think about the possibilities that lie just beyond the doorway.

Durov holds out an arm to Samantha and escorts her out of the room first, with the two of us following close behind.

The hallway opens up into a massive room with huge floor-to-ceiling windows that span the exterior walls. The view of the city alone is breathtaking, but it's the table with hors d'oeuvres that captures my attention.

On a large oak table lies a naked girl covered in sushi. I elbow Thane in the ribs. "I suddenly find that I'm starving. How about you?"

Heading over to the table, I pick up a pair of chopsticks as I admire the girl. Her pale skin is decorated with artfully placed leaves that hold the colorful hors d'oeuvres covering her body.

"Well, hello there, darlin'. Mighty fine sashimi you got there." I deliberately pick a piece off her breast and place it in my mouth, groaning in pleasure as I savor it.

I see her chest rising and falling in little bursts. She's trying hard not to laugh, which just encourages me more.

I look at the area between her legs. "What fine nigiri you have. Let me sample a bite." Deftly picking up a piece laying on her mound, I slowly chew it with a sigh of ecstasy.

"Ah, yes, darlin'. You definitely have the finest nigiri I've ever tasted."

She continues to stare up at the ceiling, her lips twitching as she struggles not to laugh.

"You *do* realize she's not allowed to move—not even a smile," Thane says, picking up a piece of sushi from her stomach. "Are you trying to get the girl punished?"

Durov slaps me on the back. "Maybe the cattleman has a sadistic streak, after all."

An older gentleman walks up beside me. "I see you are enjoying the hors d'oeuvres."

"I am, sir. Can't say I've ever seen hors d'oeuvres served in such an attractive manner, but I'm certainly a fan."

He smiles, holding out his hand to shake mine. "I like a man who appreciates Nyotaimori."

Gesturing to another naked girl smiling at me with a tumbler in her hand, he asks, "Perhaps you would like a drink?"

Before I can answer, Durov interrupts. "Mr. Everett, I'd like to formally introduce you to Master Brad Anderson, the man I spoke about."

"It's an honor to have you join us tonight, Master Anderson. I know my daughter is anxious to meet you."

I'm a little shocked to learn the man's daughter is in attendance, but who am I to judge? Must be freeing to be that open about sex within a family. "I look forward to meeting her, Mr. Everett."

"Oh, you can call me John," he says casually.

Holy shit! John Everett is one of the biggest producers in Hollywood.

Trying to keep my wits about me, I introduce Thane to him. "John, this is my friend, Thane Davis."

Instead of shaking his hand, John shakes his finger at Thane. "Wait. Aren't you the kid on the news who wants his mother killed?"

I can tell Thane has to bite back his anger when he answers. "No, but I *am* the son of Alonzo Davis, the world-renowned violinist."

John tilts his head, looking at him strangely.

Durov comes over and clasps Thane's shoulder, addressing John Everett directly. "You, more than anyone else, know you can't believe what you hear in the news." Squeezing Thane's shoulder, he adds, "Sir Thane Davis is like a brother to me."

Nodding slowly, John seems to accept Durov's assurance. "I'm glad to have you join us tonight, Sir Davis. I hope you find the night's festivities entertaining and educational."

John's gaze drifts over to Samantha and remains

glued on her. "And who is this?"

"This is Mistress Clark," Durov states in a possessive tone.

"What a fine gem you have brought to us tonight…"

I can't help wondering if Durov is having twinges of jealousy as he watches John ogle her.

John tries to take Samantha's hand to kiss it, but she snaps her crop at him and steps back. "I have not given you permission to touch me."

Instead of being offended, John seems turned on by her actions. "Of course, Mistress. My apologies. It won't happen again."

Samantha isn't at all intimidated by the fact that this is one of the most successful men in LA. No, the girl has John Everett groveling at her feet.

John regains his composure when a flirty young blonde comes bouncing up to him and begs sweetly, "Daddy, aren't you going to introduce me?"

I suck in a breath when she turns around. I can't believe Angela Laine is standing in front of me. She's only the hottest actress in all of Hollywood.

Hugging her father's arm tightly, Angela bats those big blue eyes at me while twirling a strand of her golden hair.

"Of course, princess."

Addressing me formally, he states, "Master Brad Anderson, I would like you to meet my daughter."

She blushes as she bites her bottom lip. "My name is bunny, and I want to feel your bullwhip."

I hold my breath for a moment as I reconcile the fact that this famous actress is begging for me—in front of her father, no less—to whip her.

"It's a pleasure to meet you, bunny."

Her eyes are riveted to the miniature bullwhip at my side. "Thank you, sir."

I place my finger under her chin and lift her head up to meet my gaze. "If you want to feel the bite of my whip, you are required to address me as Master."

I watch an excited shudder go through her before she slowly sinks to the floor and kneels at my feet.

John looks at his daughter with a proud glint in his eye. "Bunny will escort you to the room."

I glance over at Thane, not quite believing my luck as bunny takes my hand and guides me to one of the doors.

Bunny opens it, revealing a room of mirrors. They even cover the high ceiling above us.

"I had Daddy clear it out so it's just me, you, and…" Her eyes fall on Myrtle. "…the whip."

Needing something to bind her to, I scan the area and notice a large eye screw hanging down from the ceiling directly in the center. That will work…

"Have you ever experienced a bullwhip before?" I ask before we begin.

She looks at me sadly and shakes her head. "No one has been brave enough to whip me."

I can certainly understand why. One false move and you've just scarred a famous star. God only knows what the consequences would be if that happened.

Thankfully, I have full confidence in my skill and feel no qualms about scening with the beautiful Angela Laine.

"You understand about safewords?"

"Of course."

Bunny is much too soft a sub name for the experience I plan for her, so I spontaneously decide to change her title. "Then undress for me, slave."

Her eyes grow wide and I watch in stunned silence as she runs to the door.

Maybe "slave" was a bit much for her.

But, instead of leaving, she calls out, "He's going to do it!"

Angela immediately returns. "I'm sorry, Master," she squeaks excitedly. "It's just that this is so thrilling for me."

Normally, I would punish a sub for failing to heed my command, but I understand this is an unusual situation when the room starts filling with people.

I order them to stand against one wall to keep everyone out of the range of my whip. That's when I notice several famous faces in the crowd.

Oh, hell, now the pressure's on.

I look back at Angela and repeat my command in a low voice, "Undress, slave."

Bowing her head in reverence, she begins to undress in a slow, seductive striptease that is as much for me as it is for the crowd watching us.

My cock stirs as she reveals those firm breasts I have only dreamed about while watching her performance on the big screen.

Damn…they're even more spectacular than I imagined. I reach out to caress one, running my thumb over her hard nipple.

The idea that Angela Laine is my sub for the evening

blows my mind.

When I glance up and see some of the hottest stars on the big screen and in television staring at me expectantly, I suddenly feel a moment's hesitation.

Instead of giving in to it, I tip my hat and smile at them. I know what I'm doing. This moment is exactly what I've been practicing for.

I take in Angela Laine's naked body as she removes the last of her clothing, exposing her waxed pussy with a sexy patch of blonde pubic hair. Hot damn.

My cock aches to feel the inside of Angela Laine, but that's not what I'm here for and I forcefully redirect my thoughts. Looking at the famous television anchor standing near the door, I command, "Get me some rope."

He disappears, not even questioning my authority.

You know, I could get used to this.

Minutes later, he returns with the rope and a ladder. I appreciate the guy's initiative and thank him.

He returns to his place to watch with an eager look on his face.

Using the ladder, I take my time as I slowly pull the rope through the eye of the screw and adjust it. I enjoy making everyone wait as I get the rope ready. Once done, I fold the ladder and give it back to the man, turning to face my sub.

Her breath is already coming in short gasps, and I haven't even begun yet.

"Come to me," I command in a husky voice.

She takes in a deep breath before walking toward me. I can tell she's nervous, which only adds to the thrill of this scene.

I turn her toward the farthest wall so she can see herself and the people watching her. I slowly run my hands over the curve of her breasts and the swell of her hips, enjoying the feel of her virgin skin.

Leaning forward, I ask, "Do you want marks?"

She gasps, her breath coming more rapidly when she answers. "I do, Master."

"Nothing permanent," a short woman barks from the crowd. "And nothing she can't easily cover up."

I look over at the woman, irritated that she's interrupting our scene. "And you are?"

"Her agent."

"Ah…"

I return my focus to Angela. I can understand why she needs this—her life is not her own.

I lift Angela's arms and secure her wrists with the rope.

"Do you see how beautiful you are right now, slave?"

She nods, biting her lip when I reach for the whip at my side. Still coiled, I bring it to her lips. "Kiss her."

I watch Angela's sensual lips kiss the leather that is about to caress her skin with its bite, and I groan in her ear.

"Oh, Master…" she moans, swaying in her bonds.

I move away and unfurl it. Nobody knows who I am or what I can do, so I show them with a short demonstration, cracking Myrtle several times before I make her dance. She cuts through the air, singing her unique melody as I swing her over my head, behind me, and finish up by cracking her in rapid succession.

Afterward, the room is silent—I have everyone's full attention now.

It starts with the sound of one person clapping, and soon the entire room echoes with applause. More people try to crowd into the room, but I order the door shut.

I will allow no further distractions during my session with Angela Laine.

"First, I will warm up your skin, slave," I explain in a low, sultry tone.

She looks in the mirror, her gaze meeting mine.

Instead of lightly licking her skin to begin with, I give her a lash that hints of things to come.

She cries out, a virgin to Myrtle's demanding caress.

"Color?"

Angela says nothing.

"Color, slave?" I ask in a firmer tone.

She stares at me. In the reflection in the mirror, her eyes sparkle with anticipation. "That is wickedly erotic! I want more."

When I don't move, she quickly adds, "Green, Master."

I give her another lash of similar intensity and she cries out again. "More, more…"

She is a greedy girl, and I want to teach her patience, so I let Myrtle fly, snapping it right next to her left ear.

The terrified scream Angela lets out has her agent running forward to stop me.

"One more step and the session stops *now*," I snarl at the woman. "I will not risk an accident."

"Leave!" Angela screams at her. "Don't you dare ruin this for me."

The tiny woman glares at us both but makes her way out of the room.

"Forget that ever happened," Angela begs. "Please, Master."

I understand that she needs this even more than she knows, so I return to my position and let Myrtle fly, warming Angela's skin before I take her down the path of sensual pain.

No one in the room says a word as they listen to her impassioned screams and watch her squirm against the rope as she waits for each lash to fall, but she never cries—not one tear.

Alternating the strength of each stroke, I keep her focused on me and teach Angela Laine the allure of my bullwhip as I build up her confidence to take more.

"I admire your spirit, slave."

"Thank you, Master."

When I feel she is finally ready, I leave the first mark.

Angela starts whimpering afterward, but she still doesn't cry.

"Color?"

"Green, Master. I need this."

I understand. There is freedom in the release of emotions that a skillful whipping can provide.

Fulfilling Angela's wish, I thoughtfully place each mark. No one else will see them, but she will feel their sting as she moves about her day—and remember this moment.

Before I end our session, I move close to her and whisper, "Where would you like the final lash to fall? This one will hurt more than the others."

She turns her head toward me, her eyes flashing with anticipation. "On my ass, Master."

I caress her right cheek exactly where it will land. "So be it."

I return to my position and announce for the benefit of those gathered, "Slave, I am well pleased. Now, for your reward."

I let the whip fly, hitting her right cheek hard enough that it ripples from the impact—but without breaking the skin.

Angela cries out in a mixture of pleasure and pain.

I return to her again, nuzzling her neck as I privately compliment her on her first session with the bullwhip.

Having been tear-free during the entire scene, I'm surprised to see tears in her eyes now as she confesses breathlessly, "You can't know what this means to me."

"It was my pleasure, slave."

She laughs softly. "I never thought I would respond to that term, but when it comes from those sexy lips of yours…"

I lean down and kiss her, both of us feeling the sexual tension the bullwhip has inspired.

"I would like to repay you, Master. If you would be so kind as to untie me." She looks at me with her sultry blue eyes.

I untie her wrists and she instantly kneels at my feet. "May I?" she asks, looking at the substantial bulge in my leather pants.

There is no way I can deny her at this point, so I nod.

She undoes the button, then slowly unzips my pants.

Her blue eyes grow wide when she sees just how big my cock really is.

I hear several gasps from the crowd.

Undeterred by my size, she takes it in both hands and starts running her tongue over the head of my shaft. I groan, my cock growing even harder with her skillful attention.

Angela motions some of her friends to join her, and I suddenly find myself savoring the attention of multiple mouths.

Thank God I've learned some level of self-control or I would have come in a matter of seconds and missed out on this fucking moment.

I look down, groaning in ecstasy as three women lick, nibble, and suck my cock in front of an audience. When I finally can't take any more, I'm overcome with the overwhelming urge to shout, "There she blows!" as I climax.

Thankfully, my serious side wins out and I refrain.

Instead, I let out a roar of pleasure as my cock surges with an epic ejaculation and I hear the girls squeal in delight. I watch with rapt attention as they lick my shaft, and each other, clean.

I'm definitely going to owe Durov for this one.

Revelations

Apparently, Angela needs no aftercare. After formally thanking me for the session, she grabs her clothes and takes off with her friends to chatter about the scene. As I clean my whip, I answer questions from those in attendance.

Afterward, I seek out my friends.

I find Thane in the room across from mine. He's watching a scene with a sub and a Domme that involves fire play, and he seems completely fascinated by it. When the Domme asks if anyone would like to try it under her supervision, he instantly volunteers.

I have to hand it to Thane. He's always trying new things, no matter how risky. I personally think fire play is far more dangerous than any bullwhip.

I stay to watch as he takes off his jacket and rolls up his sleeves while the Domme explains what to do. She then dips one large swab into the jar of alcohol before handing it to him.

Thane draws an invisible line down the middle of the

naked girl's back with the alcohol, then the Domme hands him the burning swab.

"Tap and swipe it away," she instructs.

Thane nods, tapping the flame against the trail he's just created. Fire races up the girl's back. Then, with his bare hand, he swipes the flames away.

Afterward, he looks over at the Domme, the exhilaration on his face easy to see. After several more successful tries, the Domme takes a step back.

In typical Thane fashion, instead of diving right in, he hands the swabs to the Domme and leans down to speak with the sub on the table. None of us can hear what he's saying, but I see the sub smile and nod her head.

He takes the alcohol swab back, running a trail from the inside of her knee all the way up to her ass. He waits a few seconds before taking the other swab and lighting the alcohol on fire. The flame races up her leg and hovers on her ass. Thane's hand follows the trail in one smooth motion as he swipes the fire from her leg, then spanks away the last of the flames on her ass.

He moves to her other leg and repeats the process, lighting her up for all of us to admire. Then he gets a wicked glint in his eye as he runs the alcohol up the insole of her foot. Her toes wiggle from the ticklish cold, and then he taps it with the fire. She squeals as the flames caress the sensitive sole of her foot before Thane swipes them away.

"Would you like to try that again?" he asks.

"Yes. If it pleases you."

"It does," he growls huskily.

Thane teases her other foot with his fire play, making her squeal again. Afterward, he touches every area he's caressed with the flames. Then he quietly thanks the sub and turns to the Domme.

"I am indebted to you, Mistress Blaze."

She smiles. "I can see you have a natural affinity for fire play. Should you want further instruction, please don't hesitate to contact me."

Thane gathers his jacket and gives her a nod before walking over to me. I can tell he's still buzzing from the scene so we walk out of the room, so we won't disturb the others.

"Into fire, are you, buddy?"

"It's a rush!"

"You'll never catch me near flames, but I have to hand it to you. You showed absolutely no fear in there."

"Only because Mistress Blaze was beside me. It's the most dangerous BDSM play I've ever tried, but wow. That's definitely part of the thrill."

"I've never seen you this pumped up before." Clapping him on the back, I add, "But don't ever ask me to help you practice."

He raises an eyebrow. "That reminds me...you still owe me for that practice session with the bullwhip."

"Trust me, I haven't forgotten. I've been expecting you to cash in every day since."

He glances at me with a slight grin. "I'm waiting for the perfect opportunity. No reason to squander it."

I shake my head. "Lesson learned. Never agree to a simple bet with you. All I asked you to do was take a couple of lashes for me and, somehow, I think the payment is going to far outweigh that simple request."

"I wholeheartedly agree," he says with a smirk.

Nodding toward the other rooms, I ask, "Why don't we find out what's happened to Durov and Samantha?"

"Yes. I'm curious what Durov is doing…"

Thane and I have no idea what we're walking into when we enter the crowded room and immediately stop in our tracks.

In the center of the room, Durov is circling Samantha, holding a cane in his hand. He has an intense look in his eye. Samantha, however, has a look of defiance—which isn't surprising, considering she's a dominant through and through.

"I will make you like it," Durov assures her.

"It's not in my nature to submit to any man."

"But it is…" he insists, "if it's me."

She sighs, not convinced, but it's obvious she's hungry for him by the look in her eyes. She can't take them off the man.

"Where is the harm in exploring the possibility?"

"Damn it, Rytsar. You're dangerous for me."

"Am I?" He grins innocently, taking her hand and slowly pulling her to him. "I disagree." His lips lands on hers, and the two become lost in each other for a moment. When they break away, both seemed a little dazed.

The chemistry between the two is amazingly strong, but both of their personalities are incredibly domineering. It's like watching two heavyweight champions assessing each other before a fight.

"Come, Samantha. Imagine the thrill of trying something new."

Durov effectively weaves his spell, breaking down her defenses, and I can tell her resolve is starting to falter.

"I can't submit," she insists.

His lips curve into a smile. "Nothing is stopping you."

When she begins to shake her head, he grabs the back of her neck and kisses her forcefully. She responds to him, making it such a passionate kiss that I get aroused just watching it.

I glance over at Thane, who watches them with interest.

"What would you require?"

"Your complete submission." He nibbles her earlobe.

"What would be in it for me?" she asks breathlessly.

"Me."

She smirks. "You're arrogant."

"It's only arrogance if I cannot fulfill my promise to you."

"Which is…?"

"I will show you a part of yourself that you never knew existed."

She looks down at the cane in his hand and asks in a dismissive tone, "With that?"

Durov grins wickedly. "Not just with that."

Samantha stares at him without saying a word, studying his eyes for several moments. "I can quit the scene at any time?"

His grin widens. "I only want your willing submission, Mistress."

She raises an eyebrow at his use of her title.

Durov leans forward, getting dangerously close to her lips. "I will leave you…begging for more."

"If I do this, will you submit to me?"

He smirks. "*Nyet.*"

She tilts her head, frowning. "How is that fair?"

"It's not about what's fair. It's about what I can do for you—something no one else can."

The allure of his proposal is something she can't refuse, but the Dominant in her still fights against it. In her defense, submitting to another Dominant isn't something *I* could do, either.

That's why I'm surprised when Samantha walks over to the spanking bench and leans against it. With that skintight catsuit and those high heels, it is a sexy pose. Her ass is just begging to be spanked.

Looking back at him, she demands, "Hurt me, Rytsar."

His chuckle is low and alluring when he answers, "That is not how it works."

"How, then?" she asks with a seductive smile.

"Stand and let me look at my plaything for the evening."

Samantha stands up slowly and crosses her arms, still wrestling with the power exchange this requires from her.

"Hands at your sides in a submissive stance," Durov commands.

Samantha takes a deep breath but uncrosses her arms and rests them at her sides with her palms open.

Walking over to her, Durov states, "The outfit is flattering, but must go." He slowly begins undressing her until she stands before him completely naked.

"Better," he compliments her.

With scrutinizing eyes, he assesses her, touching her long blonde hair before fisting it and tugging it back, lifting her chin. "Your hair is useful for added control."

He stares intently at her mouth. "You have sensual lips."

Letting her hair go, he continues assessing her by grazing his hand over the curve of her ass before slapping it hard.

Samantha chokes down her cry of surprise, making only the slightest of sounds.

"Firm, with some pleasant give to it."

Moving to her front, he reaches out and cups her breast. "Natural. A satisfying handful for a man like me." He then brushes her nipple with his fingers, making it harder. "Are you sensitive here?"

"Somewhat."

"Good," he growls lustfully, tugging on her nipple. "I will enjoy testing your limits."

Durov smirks as he slips his finger between her legs. "I can tell you like me touching you by how wet you are." He pulls his finger from her pussy and rubs her juices against her bottom lip before kissing her deeply. Afterward, he murmurs, "Your taste is intoxicating."

She licks her red lips in answer and smiles.

"Overall, I am pleased with my plaything," he announces to everyone in attendance. Turning back to her, he adds, "Now, to find out what she's made of. Bow to your Master."

I watch in silent wonder as Samantha slowly lowers herself to her knees before him.

"All the way."

She presses her forehead to the floor; her palms face down before her.

"Take in this moment," he commands.

Durov is truly masterful in his ability to make her fully embrace her role as a submissive. It is a slow progression.

He is conditioning her mind to give up control, but he's doing it with a sexual undertone that inspires an even greater desire for him.

The man is an evil genius.

I watch Durov put her through her paces, keeping her focused on him at all times. Their unusual power exchange is erotic to watch because of the intense war of wills involved. The Russian meticulously breaks down her barriers with each task he presents her. However, he doesn't do it through pain as I was expecting he would as a sadist.

Instead, he is sensual in his dominance over her, demanding more of her with each command, but centering it on his insatiable need for her.

He doesn't pick up the cane until he has her craving his dominance.

"Do you want me to hurt you?"

"Yes," she pleads.

"And if I refuse to?"

She closes her eyes and pauses a moment before answering. "I will accept it without question."

"Why?"

She looks up at him and smiles. "Your pleasure is my pleasure."

I can tell Durov is affected by her answer because the entire mood in the room changes. There is a charge in the air when he orders her to return to the spanking bench.

It feels as if we are all one, drawn in by their intimate exchange.

My cock hardens as he positions her on the bench, her torso against the wood with her legs spread wide. Even from a distance, I can see she is extremely wet.

Durov stands beside her and raises his cane. "You are allowed to cry out. In fact, I encourage it."

I hold my breath momentarily, waiting for the cane to fall. I hear it whip through the air before it lands on her ass. She yelps but does not cry.

Rytsar leans down and tells her, "When I am finished, you will not be able to stop the tears. *That* is when I will make you come."

She nods in understanding.

"What do you want?" he asks her, his cane raised.

"I want to cry, Rytsar."

Rytsar smiles to himself as he gets back into position. I watch in stunned admiration as he unleashes his passion on her, revealing the sadist inside him.

He builds the sexual tension as he ruthlessly brings her to the edge again and again. By the time he is done, her pristine ass is covered in angry red stripes.

Samantha looks up at him unashamedly as the tears roll down her cheeks.

"You are beautiful when you cry."

She smiles through her tears.

"And now, you will experience an orgasm only I can give you." Durov reaches between her legs and teases her clit, rubbing it vigorously.

We all watch as he plays with her, building up her climax. I know he is close when she suddenly stiffens.

The room is silent as we listen to the wet sounds of Durov's vigorous manipulation. Her entire body begins to shake violently just before she screams out in pleasure. I have to look away before I come in my own damn pants.

Holy hell, that was hot!

But, Durov isn't done.

He picks Samantha up and asks John Everett, "Where's the master bedroom?"

"All the way to the end of the hall," John answers, his eyes glinting with unfulfilled lust as he watches the two head out into the hall.

Thane and I look at each other, shaking our heads.

Only Durov would have the balls to fuck in the host's own bed—and get away with it.

Meeting the Family

The day before we leave for Colorado, Durov fights through the crowd of reporters in order to chat with us while we finish packing for the trip.

"It's a fucking madhouse down there," he complains. "I don't know how you stand it."

"One day at a time," Thane answers, chuckling sadly.

"How are my men working out for you, comrade?"

"They have been tireless and effective at keeping the reporters in check. Truth is—they've saved my sanity."

Durov slaps him on the back. "I knew they would prove invaluable. It pays to surround yourself with hired protection."

"Now that I have a lawyer representing me, I shouldn't need them much longer."

"Hopefully, you'll be able to return to the dungeon once we get back," I tell Thane. "I've been missing hanging out there."

"You know you can go without me," he chides.

"No, buddy. It would feel the same as if I were to

date your girlfriend. It just wouldn't feel right to me."

"I'll make sure they take him back," Durov assures me. "It hasn't been the same there without you two."

"Hey, I almost forgot." I pull out a can from my closet and toss it to the Russian.

"What's this?" he asks, looking surprised.

"Just my little gift to you since I won't be around for Christmas."

He examines the can with a smirk. "Freeze-dried pickles?"

"Yeah, crazy, huh? I'd never seen them before, but they instantly made me think of you."

"What would freeze-dried pickles even taste like?" Thane asks, laughing.

Durov looks at the can again, shaking it. "I can't imagine, comrade."

"Why don't you open it and find out?" I suggest, curious what Durov's reaction will be.

"Why not?" he states as he pulls off the lid and a green snake erupts from the can.

With lightning speed, Durov throws the can across the room and both he and Thane jump back from the snake.

I start laughing, pointing at Durov. "That was priceless, man! Something I'll never forget."

The Russian looks down at the snake on the floor, then glares at me.

Oh, hell, I've just pissed off the sadist. I'm in for it now...

I glance over at Thane and see he's struggling not to laugh.

Durov shakes his head slowly, his gaze locked on mine.

"It was just a joke. You know…between friends."

His face gets red if he's building toward an explosion, but he surprises me when he suddenly bursts out laughing. "You're funny, cattleman. Extremely foolish…but funny."

I flash him a grin, relishing the high that comes from a well-played prank.

Thane laughs with us as he shuts his suitcase and zips it up. Walking over to Durov, he picks up the snake, handing it to him. "You'll have to let me know how this freeze-dried pickle tastes."

Durov throws the snake at me. "Ask the cattleman after I make him eat every last bite."

I go to toss the snake in the trash, but the Russian stops me. "Wait. Is that not my gift?" I hand it back to him and watch in amusement as he stuffs the snake back into the can and puts the lid back on.

Whether Durov is keeping the can to prank someone else or keeping it for himself, I'm unsure, but the Russian always manages to surprise me.

"You know, you could join us in Colorado, if you want," I offer. "Consider it payment for inviting me to that private party with Angela Laine."

Durov throws his head back and laughs. "*Nyet*, I'm no country boy." He pats me on the back. "But you have fun in the snow, freezing your balls off."

"Don't worry, we will," Thane tells him.

"You bet we will," I agree. "There's nothing like the majestic Rocky Mountains and my Ma's cooking to soothe a ravaged soul."

"An added bonus will be distancing myself from the constant hounding of the press," Thane says, looking out the window. "Did you hear the latest? I supposedly hired a hit man to take the Beast out while she's in prison. Now, she lives in constant fear for her life and is begging to be moved to a new facility." He shakes his head. "She's definitely up to something."

"I could take her out while you're gone," Durov offers with a straight face.

"Yeah, we already talked about that, my friend," he chuckles. "Promise me you'll keep your nose clean while I'm gone."

"I'll make no such promise," he answers, grinning wickedly.

"Hey, Durov, will you be spending Christmas with Samantha this year?" I pipe up, curious how much their relationship has progressed after that intense encounter at the private party.

"*Nyet.* She will be spending it with her family, just like you. But she told me she plans to share her interest in the lifestyle with them."

"You've got to hand it to Samantha, she isn't afraid of anything," Thane states with admiration. "Not even her own family."

"She is an admirable woman—in many ways," Durov agrees.

"And, hotter than hell," I add. "That scene you two did together…holy shit."

Durov grins. "It was one of my best."

Thane asks in a serious tone, "How was Samantha

afterward?"

"She was confused once the sub high wore off," Durov answers. "It was hard for her to admit to herself that she had a submissive side, and it shocked her even more that she enjoyed being on that side of the power exchange."

"Do you think she'd do it again?" I ask him.

"We will see," Durov replies, laughing. "Samantha is a complicated woman."

"So, has she asked you to submit to her?"

"Multiple times."

"Are you considering it?"

"*Nyet.* It's a hard limit."

"Interesting," Thane states. "I can see the benefit of every Dominant taking on that role at least once to better understand and experience the dynamics from the other side."

"I am not wired that way," Durov states emphatically. "I could never do it."

I chuckle, knowing how Samantha is. "I bet that frustrates the hell out of her."

The Russian smirks. "Yes, and it pleases the sadist in me."

"I bet it does." I grin.

"I suppose I should cancel future lessons with Samantha now that the two of you are getting more serious," Thane states.

"*Nyet.* Samantha still has much to learn, and I trust you as her instructor."

Thane nods, then turns to me. "Are you still good with glee helping me teach her?"

"Of course. Glee's a free spirit. It's one of the things I like most about her."

"How is it going with her?" Durov asks me.

"Actually, I was just about to head off to meet her."

"Things are going well then, cattleman?"

"Well enough, I'd say. I feel this separation will be a turning point for us. Either she'll miss me like I miss her, or we'll be indifferent."

"And if she is and you're not?" Durov asks.

"I'll cut my losses."

"So, you're not in love with her?"

I smile at him, admitting, "The possibility is there. I just haven't quite made the leap yet."

"It's wise to be cautious," Thane agrees. "There's no reason to open yourself up to potential loss."

"My parents would disagree with you," I chuckle.

"But they are the exception to the rule. The kind of love they have is rare and unattainable," he insists. "Not something to aspire to unless you want to set yourself up for failure."

I stare at him in shock. "I don't think I've realized what a cynic you truly are."

Thane shrugs. "After seeing what love did to my father, how can I feel any other way?"

I shake my head and state vehemently, "You can't go by your own parents, buddy. Your mother is *anything* but normal."

"Don't waste your breath trying to convince him about love," Durov advises. "As long as you and glee are solid, that's all that matters to me. I don't want to be the only one suffering with the complications that females bring."

Thane holds his hands up. "And, thankfully, I won't ever have to worry about that."

I chuckle to myself.

Just you wait, buddy…just you wait.

I meet glee in the outdoor commons. I want to show her around the campus to share a little of my personal life with her—something I haven't done before. I want glee to be certain of my growing feelings for her, especially with me leaving LA for a month.

I can't help whistling as she walks toward me wearing a blue summer dress this time. Just as before, glee's dress gives her a deceptively innocent look.

I'm fond of her many facets—in and out of the dungeon.

"Hey, darlin'."

"Hello, handsome," she cries, running up to me. She stands on tiptoes to give me a kiss on the cheek, but I wrap my arms around her and pull her close, planting a deep kiss on those sweet lips.

"Is that a present, I see?" she asks coyly, staring at the box in my hand.

I look down at the wrapped gift with a red bow, and smile. "Since I won't be here for Christmas, I thought I would give it to you early."

She looks at me with a worried expression. "I didn't think ahead. I don't have anything for you, Master

Anderson."

"Don't give it a second thought, darlin'. And it's Brad," I remind her with a wink.

She giggles. "Oops! Sorry."

"No apologies necessary," I assure her, stealing another kiss.

I hand her the present, anxious for her to open it. "It's a small thing I had made for you."

"You had it made for me?" she squeals, tearing at the paper. When she lifts the lid, she murmurs, "Oh, my goodness!"

Picking it up, she examines the bracelet closely.

"The craftsman who made my bullwhip used the same type of leather to create it."

Her eyes sparkle with joy. "Brad, this is so special."

I take the braided leather and put it around her small wrist, fastening it. "I wanted to give you something to remind you that I'm thinking of you."

Glee wraps her arms around me. "I didn't realize you were such a romantic."

"I try to keep that under wraps. It kind of messes with the whole big, bad Dom image."

Smiling up at me, she says, "No, it doesn't. It makes you an even better Dom in my eyes."

I have a good feeling about us. Touching the bracelet around her delicate wrist, I confess, "I'm going to miss you."

"I'm going to miss you, too." She stands on her tiptoes again and whispers, "Master."

Hearing her call me by my title has a definite effect on my libido, and that doesn't go unnoticed by glee.

Glancing down at my "growing" attraction, she murmurs, "Why don't we find a quiet place?"

"I would take you to my dorm room, but it's swimming with reporters. No way could I sneak you in without them noticing."

"You know…I *do* like the thrill of public places," she says with a flirtatious glint in her eye.

"If you're looking for someplace quiet, I know the perfect place, darlin'."

I take her hand and head to the quietest place I know—the college library.

Twelve hours later, I'm on a plane, socking Thane in the arm as we land in Denver. "Would you look at that? Seriously, is there anything more beautiful?" I ask him, pointing at the snow-covered mountain range in the distance.

"The peaks are impressive."

"You've got that right, buddy. Colorado has fifty-three fourteeners."

"I'm sorry. I have no idea what that means."

I chuckle, surprised he doesn't know. "Fourteeners are peaks that are 14,000 feet or higher."

Thane nods as if it means nothing to him.

I chuckle at his level of ignorance. Nodding toward the mountains, I explain, "People come from all over the world to take on the challenge of scaling them all."

"Ah."

Seeing he's still not impressed, I mention, "I've climbed twelve of them myself."

The plane rolls to a stop and the two of us stand up, waiting for people to start exiting. I elbow him in the ribs. "Hey, maybe you and I can make it an annual thing. You come to Colorado every year, and we'll climb one. Just think, fifty-three years from now, we'll have climbed them all."

Thane chuckles. "Do I look like a hiker to you?"

"I'm telling you, buddy. There's nothing else like it. It's just you and the mountain. Have you ever spent a night under the stars with no one else around?"

"Can't say I have."

"It's an incredible feeling," I tell him, thinking back fondly on all the trips I've taken. "You can walk as far as you want, camp wherever you want. Talk about experiencing true freedom." I nudge him as he goes to grab his luggage from the overhead. "Food never tastes as good as it does in the mountains after a day of hiking—doesn't matter what it is."

"I'll have to take your word for it."

"And fire. You can't have an appreciation for it until it becomes your source of life."

As we start moving down the aisle toward the exit, Thane says, "Sounds like it's had a real impact on you."

"It would be the same for you. You haven't really lived until you've spent a weekend in the mountains, living in harmony with nature while you take in all the beauty she has to offer."

"I think I'll pass."

I bump against him as we walk up the jetway. "I would hate for you to go through your entire life having never lived."

He gives me an amused look. "It would be a tragedy, wouldn't it?"

I snort, promising myself that come hell or high water, I'm getting Thane back out here in the summer so he can experience the thrill of backpacking in the majestic Rockies.

The first people I see when we get to the main terminal are my parents. I'd already explained to them that Thane needs to remain incognito while in Colorado, so there isn't a giant crowd waiting to meet us.

No, this time, it's just a small portion of my family.

"Those must be your sisters," Thane states. "They all have same dark hair and green eyes you do."

I smile as my sisters start waving at us enthusiastically.

What looks like a small gathering to me seems to overwhelm my friend, and he slows his pace. "Are they all here for you?"

"For us, buddy," I tell him, placing my hand on his back and pushing him forward.

My sisters break rank and run over to us, hugging me and gushing over Thane—Megan especially. I give her a discreet wink, approving of her tactics.

I then introduce Thane to my parents. Thane nods to them. "Thank you for having me."

My pop huffs, "What kind of greeting is that? I'm insulted."

Thane looks confused and glances at me with a concerned expression, before apologizing to my father. "I'm sorry, sir."

Pop walks over and holds out his arms. "We're family here."

Thane stammers something as my father envelops him in a hug. The look on Thane's face is comical. I guess the poor guy isn't used to hugs—but he soon will be!

My mother gives him a hug next. "I can't tell you how excited I've been knowing you were coming to visit us for Christmas."

I see Thane flinch when she mentions the holiday, but he forces a smile. "I'm grateful for the invitation."

"You're safe here with us," she tells him.

Thane's eyes flash with a look I haven't seen before, and I can tell he's moved.

My mother turns to my grandparents. "Let me introduce you to Grandma Kelly and Granddad Jacob."

Thane shakes my grandma's hand stiffly. It seems so awkward, when hugs are the norm in our family. "It's a pleasure to meet you."

He looks to my granddad next. "I'm grateful your grandson shared your fine whiskey with me."

My granddad grins. "You enjoyed it, did you?"

"I did, sir."

"Put 'er there, boy." When Thane goes to shake his hand, my grandfather grabs him in a hug. "Shaking hands is for strangers."

Thane glances over at me, clearly uncomfortable. He needs this trip more than he knows—and it has nothing to do with avoiding the press.

After getting our luggage, we head out. Thane and I have the privilege of driving in Pop's old Chevy truck while the rest of my family crowds into the minivan.

Throwing our luggage in the back of the Chevy, I

open the door for Thane and tell him to jump in.

He hesitates when he sees the interior.

I chuckle. "Have you ever ridden in one of these before?"

"No."

"It's called a bench seat. Scoot in, buddy. Things are about to get a lot more intimate. I'd take the middle seat, you being a guest and all, but you're shorter and Pop needs to be able to reach the gearshift."

Thane crawls inside. I watch with amusement as my pop reaches between Thane's legs to put the car in reverse, telling him, "Welcome to country living."

As we head down the highway toward Greeley, Thane looks around stating, "I expected there to be snow."

"Sorry to disappoint you, son. We've had a particularly warm winter this year. Unusually so," my father informs him.

Thane gets an odd look on his face.

"No reason to fret," my father laughs. "I'm sure Mother Nature will come through and give us a white Christmas."

I'm curious about what's got Thane so bothered and think back on what my father said. I realize it must be because he said "son."

It's a common word my father uses when talking to any young man he respects, but I can see it has had an effect on Thane.

I can't imagine losing Pop at fifteen—can't even allow myself to think about it. Thane carries burdens that no one sees. I hope, somehow, this month with my family will help ease the weight of those burdens.

Christmas in Colorado

That night, we gather around the kitchen table for our first meal together, and I feel a sense of pride as I look over the spread my mother has set out. The table is loaded with our family favorites—thick, succulent steak, creamy mashed potatoes, buttery corn on the cob, steamed green beans, and Ma's killer homemade rolls. A veritable feast, by any man's standards!

Thane sits beside me and smiles at my sisters across the table. Megan blushes and then giggles, then sneaks another peek across the table and giggles some more.

Damn, she's doing a good job playing the flirtatious sister.

Thane's not sure what to makes of that and looks at me uncomfortably. Little does he know; she's just getting started.

Pop starts the meal by passing around the platter of steak, before sending around the other dishes. Soon, all of our plates are full, but I see Thane hasn't completely filled his. The guy doesn't have nearly enough mashed potatoes, so I add an extra spoonful to his plate and throw on an extra roll. "No need to be shy around here, buddy. Ma always makes enough for seconds."

Thane holds up one of the rolls, admiring its perfect shape and color. He then nods to my mother. "Thank you, Mrs. Anderson. This looks delicious."

Her green eyes sparkle. "It's made with love. Please enjoy."

Before Thane can take a bite, my father clears his throat and my family takes one another's hands.

Thane looks around the table and quickly sets down his roll, taking my hand and that of my father's before bowing his head.

Pop looks at Thane and smiles before bowing his own head to say the blessing. "Dear Lord, we are grateful for your bounty. May every bite fill and nourish our family so we can go out and honor You with our deeds. Thank you for bringing Brad's friend Thane home to us. We pray this is a time of renewal for both boys. Bless our family, bless this ranch, and all who live here, animal or human. We ask this in the name of Jesus Christ. Amen."

"Amen," we all echo.

"Dig in boys," Pop announces as he takes a mouthful of potatoes and lets out a groan of pleasure.

"Perfect as always, my dear," he says to my mother.

To Thane, he states with pride, "You won't find a better cook. My wife understands food better than anyone I know."

"Except for your son," my mother interjects. "Brad surpasses me."

My sisters elbow each other and giggle. They think it's hilarious that I'm the only one who inherited Ma's cooking gene, since all three of them hate to cook.

Pop looks over at me. "You are going to make a wife very happy one day, son."

"You certainly will," Ma agrees, winking at me before she takes a forkful of green beans.

Thane cuts into his meat and takes his first bite. His eyes grow wide and he smiles while he chews. After swallowing, he looks at my father in amazement. "It's so tender and unbelievably juicy. This is honestly the best steak I've ever eaten."

Pop smiles proudly, nodding. "That's what open pastures, Colorado sunshine, and humane treatment can do. You won't find better meat anywhere."

"If I wasn't a believer in your methods before, I am now," Thane states, cutting himself another bite.

"Eat up, son. It does my heart good, seeing you enjoy it."

I sit back in my chair, overwhelmed with a sense of pride for this family I've been born into.

I know Thane was concerned about coming to live with a family of strangers for a month, but I hope he can already tell that he belongs here.

Damn, I love how my father thinks when it comes to pranks!

Due to the unusually warm weather Greeley has been

experiencing, he decides to introduce Thane to a "unique" tradition in our family. The very next day, as we're sitting down to breakfast, Pop announces, "The horse stalls need a thorough cleaning. I want you boys to join me later to help."

"Sure thing, Pop," I answer, having already been told what he has in mind.

"I'd be happy to," Thane replies.

"Good. We're a working ranch. Doesn't matter what time of year it is, there's always work to be done."

Thane nods. "Understood, Mr. Anderson."

I notice my sisters throwing glances at each other during the exchange between my father and Thane. So, they've been informed about what's happening too.

Excellent!

Pop's prank gives me an idea, and I see no reason not to take advantage of this unexpected opportunity. "Hey, Megan, can I talk to you after breakfast?" I casually ask just before I shove a huge bite of Ma's buttery pancakes dripping with maple syrup, into my mouth.

She gives me a half-smile. "Of course, big brother."

I tell Thane he needs to dress in something he doesn't mind getting dirty. Once he leaves to change, I take Megan aside and explain what I'm thinking. Thankfully, my sis is totally on board and gives me a high-five.

Truly, the Anderson family is a dangerous force to unsuspecting people like Thane.

When he comes out of his bedroom, I give Thane a disapproving look. "Is that the best you can do?"

He looks down at his clothes. "What? Not good

enough?"

"Too good, buddy. We're cleaning shit, you know. Those jeans are new, aren't they?"

He shrugs. "I don't have anything else. Besides, a little dirt won't hurt them."

"Well, okay. It's your clothes…"

As we head down to the barn, I gesture to the vast amounts of yellow grass. "Normally, all this would be covered in pristine white. It's truly magical to behold."

"I'll have to take your word for it, because it all looks pretty dead to me."

"Just you wait. It will be a sight you won't forget."

I open the barn door and tell Thane to head in first.

"You're just in time, boys!" my father calls out to us.

I see Thane squint as his eyes adjust to the darkness. Then his jaw slackens, as my father comes into focus.

Yep, there my pop stands in all his naked glory, holding a rake in his hand.

"Don't just stand there, son," he tells Thane. "Grab a rake and get to work."

I grin as I whip off my clothes, even though it's a tad chilly, and head over to Hot Chocolate's stall to start clearing it out.

Glancing back, I see Thane hasn't moved from his spot, his eyes still taking in my father's well-endowed frame, which happens to match mine.

"You've got nothing to be ashamed of, buddy," I assure Thane. "Remember, I've seen you naked before."

"Why do this naked?" Thane asks, looking bewildered.

"Why not?" my pop answers for me. "It's incredibly empowering to wear only what the good Lord has given you."

"Go on, buddy. Give it a try," I encourage him.

When Thane doesn't budge, I have to keep from laughing.

I walk into Hot Chocolate's stall and lead her out, wrapping her lead around the handle of the next stall as if mucking out dirty stalls in the nude is completely normal.

A few minutes later, Thane joins me in the stall—naked.

I struggle to keep my composure and manage not to blink an eye when I hand him the rake. "Let me get the shovel while you start raking it into a pile."

I look at my pop as I leave the stall, my facial muscles contorting as I fight with everything in me not to burst out laughing. Of all his pranks to date, this one definitely tops the list.

But I'm not done with Thane yet…

When we're almost done shoveling out all the stalls, I tell him. "There's a large gray hose outside just left of the barn. Could you get it?"

He hesitates for a moment, but heads to the barn door. As soon as he leaves, I move over to the left side of the barn to listen in.

First, I hear Thane clear his throat uncomfortably. "I didn't realize you would be out here."

Megan giggles. "I was just chasing one of our chickens that got loose."

He clears his throat again. "I was told to get a hose, but I can't find it."

"Oh, I think I know where it is. Let me go get it."

"That's quite all right. I can—"

I snicker when I hear Megan dragging the hose to him a few minutes later.

"Well…I was told it was a gray hose, but I'm sure this will do. Thank you."

"Gee," she says in a flirtatiously innocent voice, "it sure looks like my dad's been working you awfully hard."

"I…ah…really should get this back to your father."

"Okay. Back to it, then."

As he's walking away, Megan calls out. "Don't worry, Thane. That's a really nice hose you've got there."

I clamp my hands over my mouth, muffling my fits of laughter.

I love my sister for her cunning ability to take advantage of every opportunity while carefully building the foundation to my prank.

Thane has no clue he's being played.

After that initial introduction to our 'unique' family tradition, Thane has no idea what to think, but he doesn't question it. In fact, I notice the longer he's with us, the more relaxed he seems.

It doesn't hurt that my sisters and I keep everyone in stitches, pranking each other, egged on by his presence.

And, for all his complaints about Christmas, Thane shares a completely different side of himself on the actual day.

I knock on his door repeatedly, calling out, "Rise and shine, buddy!"

I hear him groan on the other side of the door. "It's only five in the morning."

"Christmas starts early in the Anderson household. I don't know if you've heard, but Santa snuck down our chimney last night."

He groans again. "Be gone and let me go back to sleep."

"You've got to think of the children. My poor little sister has probably been up all night, waiting to see what Santa left under the tree. You wouldn't want Christina to suffer longer than she has to just because you want to catch a few more Z's."

"Of course, not…" he grumbles.

Ten minutes later, Thane opens the door, fully dressed in a freaking suit.

I brush back my tussled hair and look down at my comfortable PJ's. "You *do* know it's only five in the morning."

"Funny," he says drolly. "This is an important occasion for your family, so I want to dress appropriately for it."

I roll my eyes as we head down the hall together. "You're an odd duck."

"Says the man who cleans stalls in the nude."

I start snort-laughing down the stairs.

My mom wants to know what's so funny, but as soon as Thane enters the room, she stops midsentence and stares at him. I glance over at my sisters and see they are equally awestruck.

Fuck Thane and his suits.

"You can stop gawking, girls," I tease my sisters.

"Haven't you ever seen a dude in a suit before?"

"Not here…" Megan says in awe.

"And not on Christmas morning," Ruthie adds.

Thane seems uncomfortable with the attention and asks my father, "Should I go change?"

But my father finds it amusing. "Not at all, son. You bring a sense of class to our home."

"You do look mighty handsome, Thane," my mother adds. She hands him a cup of coffee, explaining, "We always drink something warm before we let the chaos begin."

Thane glances over at the Christmas tree with the mountain of presents surrounding it. "That's quite an impressive tree."

Pop speaks up. "We're a family that always lives within our means. But after such a successful year, I figured it might be fun to spoil the kids for a change."

"There's certainly no harm in that," Thane agrees.

We sit down and slowly drink our coffee, as my sisters fidget in their seats, waiting impatiently for Pop to give them the word.

After he takes his last sip of coffee, he finally does, and all hell breaks loose as the girls race to the tree and start tearing at the paper.

"What were Christmases like at your house?" my father asks Thane.

"Pop…" I warn, knowing Thane doesn't want to talk about anything to do with the holiday.

"No, that's okay," Thane assures me. Watching the girls unwrap their gifts, he says, "It was much more subdued, compared to this. My mom always insisted we unwrap our gifts one at a time so each of us could appreciate every present."

"This must be unsettling for you, then," my mother states with concern.

"No, I actually prefer it." He glances at my mother and smiles. "Kids don't want to appreciate other peoples' gifts. They just want to unwrap their own."

My father chuckles. "Very true. Who wants to stifle a child's joy with adult rules?"

"Exactly," Thane agrees.

After twenty minutes of squeals, hugs, and paper flying everywhere, my sisters are finally done unwrapping their presents.

My father leaves the room for a few minutes, returning with a saddle in his arms. "For you, Brad. You've ridden that old saddle long enough."

I get up and walk over to him. Awed, I run my hands over the fine leather. "This is too much, Pop. You've given enough helping me through college."

"Nonsense, my boy. You have worked alongside me all these years. This gift is long overdue."

"I bet Rebel is going to love it," I say, turning the saddle over to admire the soft fleece underneath.

Pop raises an eyebrow. "Don't you mean Hot Chocolate?"

I look at my father, stunned. There's no way Sofia would ever have given up my secret. "How did you know?"

Pop glances over at my sisters.

I silently groan, remembering their intrusion that night in the barn. They must have overheard me when I was talking to Sofia, and then one of those stinkers spilled the beans.

"Which one of you snitched?" I demand.

"None of them. I've known for years. I thought it was funny that my brave son, the bullwhipping bull rider, called his own horse Hot Chocolate."

I look at him sheepishly. "What can I say? The name stuck."

My mother gets up and walks to the tree, coming back with a small gift with a big red bow. She hands it to Thane and explains, "Brad told us you often wear suits."

I snort, pointing at the guy. "Was I right or was I right?"

She laughs softly. "We thought this seemed appropriate. Hope you like it."

Thane gives her a genuine smile. "I'm certain I will, Mrs. Anderson."

He is meticulously slow in unwrapping the gift, driving me crazy as we all wait to see what's inside. When he finally opens it, Thane lets out an almost imperceptible gasp.

Taking out the cufflinks, he holds them up for us to see. The silver cufflinks are shaped like miniature violins.

"It's perfect," Thane says. "Thank you, everyone."

"Nicely played, you guys," I compliment my parents, liking the cleverness of my own pun.

Thane takes off the ones he's wearing and replaces them with the new ones, telling her, "On days like this, it's good to remember my father."

"He's always with you, son," my father assures him.

Thane stands up abruptly. "I have gifts for all of you in my room."

My sisters start chattering excitedly when he leaves to get them.

I must admit, I'm a bit surprised. I know Thane despises this holiday, and I'd warned my sisters that they weren't getting anything from him.

A few minutes later, Thane returns with presents in hand and walks over to the table to set them down. "We'll start with the girls first."

Thane hands each of them a similarly sized box. They waste no time ripping off the bows and paper to get to the good stuff.

"So pretty," Christina coos, lifting up a delicate necklace with a gemstone. Ruthie and Megan hold theirs up, too, each one a different color.

"I asked your mother what month you were born so I could get the correct birthstone for each of you," Thane tells them.

"Ma, put it on, put it on!" Christina cries, giving it to her and lifting her hair up.

While my mother puts on the necklace, Megan walks over to Thane. "Would you mind putting it on for me, please?"

Thane can't refuse her request but looks uncomfortable as he fastens it behind her neck. Megan glances over at me and winks.

When he's done, she turns around to face him and asks sweetly, "What do you think, Thane?"

He answers stiffly, "It looks fine."

She plays flirtatiously with the gem around her neck, telling him, "It's a beautiful gift. Thank you."

"Of course."

He glances over at Ruthie and removes himself from

the uncomfortable situation by asking her, "Would you like me to help you with that?"

"Yes, please."

I snicker to myself. Every little action and reaction with Megan are going to take on a whole new meaning soon.

I'm so funny, I slay myself.

Thane hands my mother a gift. "It's a simple thing."

The minute my mother opens her present, her face lights up. "These are extraordinary, Thane." Ma holds up an intricately decorated set of measuring spoons with painted butterflies on them.

She shows them to me, "Aren't they exquisite?"

"They are, Ma."

"I'll be sure not to ruin them," she tells Thane.

"Oh no, they are meant to be used, Mrs. Anderson," he assures her. "I asked before I bought them. I thought, since you cook every day, it might be nice to have something pretty to work with."

I've got to hand it to the guy. He really hit it home with this gift. My mom can't stop gushing.

Thane hands my Pop his gift. It turns out to be a canteen with our family name engraved on it. "This is mighty nice, son."

"I did my research, and this one has the highest rating. It's lightweight but will keep your water cold on those hot days when you're out taking care of the cattle."

Pop turns the canteen around in his hands, admiring it. "A *very* thoughtful gift. Thank you."

"Use it in good health," Thane tells him, obviously pleased my father likes the gift.

Thane then turns to me. "That just leaves you."

"It does but let me get your gift from under the tree first." I wade through all the paper and empty boxes and am relieved to see she remains untouched. I proudly carry her back to Thane and present her to him, saying, "There is nothing more satisfying or soothing than nurturing a beauty like this baby."

Thane stares at it in disbelief. "What am I going to do with a plant?"

"You're going to water her and talk to her daily."

"I don't *do* plants."

"Don't worry. I've given you one of the easiest to care for."

Thane frowns as he looks down at the potted plant.

"Look, buddy. You need something to nurture and love. Clementine, here, fits the bill."

He gives me an exasperated look. "You named the plant?"

"Of course. It helps with the bonding."

"I'm not bonding with a plant, Anderson."

"You say that now, but just you wait. In a couple of weeks, you and Clementine will be inseparable."

Thane sighs. He puts it on the table and begrudgingly thanks me for it.

"I got you something, too, but you're not required to care for it or talk to it."

I quickly rip the paper away to find a wooden box. "Fancy box…I wonder what's inside." I let out a long whistle when I see the chef's knife nestled inside. "You really shouldn't have, buddy."

"I remembered what you said about your interest in cooking, and I've heard a quality knife is an essential tool for a chef."

"It is…it certainly is," I agree, admiring the knife. I hand it over to my mom, who is equally impressed by the exceptional quality of it.

I glance at Thane's plant and joke, "Had I known you were going all out, I would have gotten you two."

Thane chuckles, picking up the plant. "Trust me. One plant is all I can tolerate."

While my sisters play with their presents, Thane and I sip on hot chocolate spiked with a touch of my granddad's whiskey and watch the sun slowly rise.

"I can't believe it snowed overnight," Thane says.

I smile as the brilliant colors in the sky compliment the white snow covering the ground. "What a perfect way to ring in Christmas morning."

"Agreed," he says with awe, as he stares at the winter landscape nature created.

I turn at him and have to chuckle. "You know, for a guy who hates Christmas, you sure did a bang-up job with the gifts.

Thane takes a long sip before answering. "I appreciated your family taking in a stranger with a past like mine. This was simply my way of expressing how much it meant to me."

"Well, you did good, buddy."

Thane takes another drink as he stares at the sunrise.

He has a far-off look in his eyes, and I'm struck again by the heavy burdens he carries in silence.

On Bended Knee

Thane points out the airplane window at the ocean and says in a mocking voice, "Would you look at that? Seriously, is there anything more beautiful?"

I elbow him in the ribs. "Nothing compares to the Rockies, buddy."

"Actually, nothing beats the sound of the waves."

I snort. "Like you ever even go near the ocean, much less, in it."

Thane chuckles. "True." He stares out the window and mutters, "But someday I'll have a place on the beach, and I'll be listening to those waves every day."

"I like that you think big," I tease.

He turns to look at me. "I'm serious."

I like the drive Thane has. It's unrelenting. Even though he's full of lofty ideas, I don't doubt he'll have a house on the beach someday.

As for myself, I envision a house in the Rockies with an entire room dedicated to BDSM play and a lone pole in the yard to practice my whipping skills. Who knows?

Maybe glee will be there with me.

As we wait to get our luggage at the baggage carousel, I confess to him, "I'm anxious to get back to glee more than anything else."

"What? Are things getting serious on your end?"

I smile to myself. "There's certainly potential there."

"You know, I find it amusing that your parents are so pushy about you finding the right girl."

"They believe in love. What can I say?"

He laughs, shaking his head. "Your father, in particular, kept insisting I'd already met the right girl, and that I just hadn't opened myself up to seeing it yet."

"My pop is relentless that way," I agree, chuckling a little too loudly. I seriously can't believe my luck. I had no idea my father had been giving Thane relationship advice during our stay.

Pop doesn't know it, but he's given me the perfect ammunition for my prank. There are times in life when everything aligns as if it is meant to be.

This is one of those times.

I look at Thane, struggling not to laugh, wondering how he will react when the anvil falls.

With a poke to my ribs, Thane asks, "What?" His raises his eyebrows, suggesting he knows something is up.

"Nothing…"

"Out with it." This time his poke actually hurts.

"Let's just say I'm glad we're here. Even though I miss my family, this is where I belong."

"The one thing I *won't* miss is cleaning the barn in the nude." He shakes his head. "That has got to be the weirdest thing I've ever done."

I can't suppress my snicker and, once it starts, there's no holding back. I burst out with a deep belly laugh. It's so contagious, the people around us start laughing, too, even though they have no idea what I'm laughing about.

The only person who is not amused is Thane. He folds his arms and demands, "What's so damn funny, Anderson?"

I counter his annoyance with a compliment, knowing I've almost let the cat out of the bag by exposing Pop's prank. Chuckling as I grab my bag from the carousal, I tell him, "Truth is, I never imagined I'd be mucking out a stall with you by my side. But I've got to hand it to you, buddy. The way you pitched in was truly inspiring."

Thane gives me a sideways glance as he grabs his suitcase.

That was close.

Even though Pop's prank was a good one, it's *nothing* compared to mine...

After getting our bags, we head outside where Durov is waiting with his chauffeur to drive us back to our dorm. I've often wondered how affluent his family is back in Russia. For a rich kid, Durov is unusually humble. He doesn't flaunt his wealth, but he also isn't ashamed of it.

I aspire to be like that someday.

"So, comrade, was cow town everything you'd hoped it would be?" he asks Thane as we climb into the vehicle.

Thane glances at me. "Let's just say it was…interesting."

I nod in agreement, grinning from ear to ear. "It certainly was."

Looking out the car window, Thane adds, "It was beneficial, getting away. Being back here, I can already feel the walls closing in."

When we arrive at the dorm, I'm stunned. There's not a single reporter in sight.

"He did it…" Thane says in amazement as he gets out of the car.

I smile. "I figured after he got me off the hook with the dean, the guy knew what he was doing."

Thane shakes his head. "Still, after everything I've suffered, I didn't think he could actually pull it off."

"You've got yourself a winner in that lawyer of yours," Durov states.

I laugh. "And, the guy works for peanuts."

"I have no idea how I'm going to repay him for this."

"You could always invite him to my beach house for a private party. Introduce the man to the BDSM lifestyle," Durov suggests with a wicked grin.

"I can just imagine Thompson all tied up, being whipped by a Domme, crying out, 'I acquit, I acquit!'" I joke.

Thane rolls his eyes. Picking up his suitcase, he heads inside the building. When we reach our room, I find an envelope addressed to me taped to the door. Pulling it off, I take it inside the room to read it.

I quickly scan the contents and smile.

"What does it say?" Thane asks.

"It's personal," I tell him, folding up the letter and sticking it in my pocket.

"Who is it from?" Durov demands.

"If you must know, it's from glee."

"Good news or bad?"

"Good," I answer. "Apparently, I've been missed."

"She's not the only one who has missed you," Durov informs me. "You'll find several subs at the dungeon have also missed the cattleman and his bullwhip."

I smile at Thane smugly.

Durov then turns to Thane, putting an arm around his shoulder. "And, there are more who pine away for you, comrade."

Thane glances at me and chuckles.

"You will be pleased to hear the dungeon has extended its welcome again to you."

Thane lets out a sigh of relief. "That *is* welcomed news. It's been too damn long."

"We should go this weekend," Durov tells us, "and remind them what they have been missing."

The next day, I grab my mail and head up to my dorm room. Flipping through the envelopes, I grin when I see the letter from my sister.

Let the fun begin…

"Hey, buddy," I say nonchalantly as I enter the room and drop the rest of the mail on my desk while I settle down to read it.

Thane glances over at me and gives me a nod before going back to his studies.

After I finish reading Megan's letter, I say, "Aww…Megan's got a crush."

Thane continues studying as if he hasn't heard me.

"You'll never guess who it is."

Thane finally looks up from his book. "Who?"

"You."

"What?" he exclaims, his voice going up an octave.

"Yeah, I guess you made quite an impression on her. She's gushing all over about you in this letter." I hold it up for him to see.

His brow furrows when he defends himself, "Trust me, Anderson. I did nothing to elicit such feelings."

"Well, apparently you did, because she's totally smitten."

Thane palms his forehead, groaning loudly.

"You know, I'd normally punch a guy for looking at my sister the wrong way."

He meets my gaze, declaring, "I have no designs on your sister. Trust me."

"Well, she certainly has strong feelings for you."

"Let me see that," he insists.

I hand Thane Megan's letter and watch as he swallows hard while reading it, looking perplexed.

"See what I mean? Megan's crushing hard."

"I…I don't even know what to say."

I keep back my smile as I take the letter from him and slip it into the envelope. "I'm sure it's nothing. She'll probably be crushing on some other guy next week."

He nods in agreement. "I trust she will."

Thane goes back to his homework, still completely oblivious that he's being played.

I have to applaud myself. The guy doesn't see it coming—just as I predicted.

Never challenge the Master of Pranks.

I finally see glee after my first day of classes. Her work schedule has recently changed, and it cuts our first reunion short.

It seems like forever since I've last held glee in my arms. "Come here," I command as she approaches. I envelop her in my arms and hug her tight.

She rests her head against my chest and sighs contentedly. "I love being in these arms."

Those simple words have an unexpected effect on me, and I suddenly have an overwhelming desire to protect her. I squeeze her tighter. "My arms are always open to you, darlin'."

We stand there for several moments, taking in each other's presence after our month-long separation.

Glee abruptly pulls away, announcing, "I have a present for you." Opening her purse, she pulls out a long, thin box. "Open it, please!"

I open the lid and see a black leather bolo tie with a stone slide. Lifting it out of the box, I admire it before slipping it over my neck and adjusting the slide. "It's perfect."

She grins, touching it lightly with her fingers. "I wanted to give you something personal, since you had something special made for me." She glances down at the bracelet around her wrist.

"So, this has a story behind it?"

"It does." She plays with the sparkling brown stone as she explains, "This is my lucky rock. I found it next to the stream where I grew up when I was twelve, and I've had it with me ever since. I decided to have this guy I know grind and polish it so you would always have a part of me."

I look down at the stone and smile. "You gave me your luck, did you?"

"I did." She glances up at me with a naughty grin. "It was partly selfish, though. You see, I've been imagining how hot you would look wearing it—and nothing else."

I growl huskily, "I wish we had more time today, but I'll be sure to wear it at the dungeon this weekend."

She shivers in delight. "I can't wait."

Lifting her chin, I give her a deep kiss that not only expresses my desire for her, but also my growing feelings.

I didn't tell my parents about glee during winter break, because I still wasn't sure if I was ready to open up to her. Based on my feelings now, however, I think a call to my parents may soon be warranted.

I now understand Durov's need to have someone to commiserate with. I feel as if I'm on a cliff, and if I dare take another step, I just might fall hard for her.

Megan's second letter arrives a week later. The day of reckoning has finally arrived…

Thane has no idea how hard it is for me to appear calm after months of planning for this day.

I hold up the letter and wave it in the air. "It's from Megan."

He appears uninterested as he goes back to writing his research paper, but I know he's paying attention.

I'd feel sorry for the guy, but he started this the day he told me I talk in my sleep.

I even warned him…

Struggling to hide my mounting excitement, I get ready for my performance of a lifetime.

I slowly scan through Megan's carefully crafted letter, feeling prouder and prouder as I read each word she's written. The girl is thorough and cunning in her delivery. For Thane's benefit, I groan loudly as I read and finish with a distressed, "Oh, no…"

Thane glances at me. "What's happened now?"

"I can't believe this." I give him a crestfallen look.

I'm pleased to note the concern in his eyes when he asks, "Is something wrong?"

Meeting his worried gaze, I confirm his fears. "It's even worse than I thought."

"What do you mean?"

"You know how I thought she had a crush on you?"

"Yes…" he answers uneasily.

I hit the letter with the back of my hand. "Buddy, the

girl's in love with you."

"She can't be," he protests.

"She can and she is."

"That's preposterous."

Looking at the letter again, I let out a wolf whistle before adding, "Well, she says you feel the same way."

Thane slaps his book closed. "I barely talked to the girl the whole time I was there."

"That's not true. I saw you talk to her every day."

His clenches his jaw. "I talked to *all* your sisters daily."

I wave the letter over my head. "Well, it's all here in black and white."

"Give me the letter," Thane demands, jumping up from his desk and grabbing it out of my hand.

The frown on his face deepens as he reads through it but, after he's done, he meets my gaze evenly, declaring, "Megan is wrong."

I put on my tough guy face and make a fist with one hand. "What? Are you calling my sister a liar?"

"No, but she misconstrued everything I said." He looks at me in desperation. "I would never…she's your sister."

"Look, if you love the girl, just admit it."

"Stop saying that word!"

"Hey, if you're worried about what my family thinks, don't be. My Pop approves."

Thane's face loses all color. "Your father approves?"

"Yeah. Apparently, he noticed your mutual attraction. He told Megan he even talked to you about it."

Thane closes his eyes, muttering, "I never thought

for a second he was talking about her."

I chuckle sadly. "Well, at least you can take consolation in the fact that my family approves."

"Approves of what?"

"If you want to make it official—get down on bended knee."

His jaw drops as his already pale face takes on a pinkish hue. "You've got to be kidding."

"You mean you don't have any feelings for her?"

He shakes his head slowly.

I give him a stricken look, backing away from him. "You're going to break Megan's heart, aren't you?"

"No, I'm not. I'm telling you, I did nothing to lead your sister on," he insists. "She must have imagined it."

I let out a long, tortured sigh. "I believe you, buddy. But it doesn't change the fact that it's going to completely crush her."

"I don't know what to do," he mutters, sitting down on his bed. "I'm totally at a loss here."

"Megan is a sensitive soul. I'd hate to think what this will do to her, and she has the family involved now."

"I know…" he says miserably. "This is unfortunate for everyone."

"At least you can take comfort in knowing they were willing to welcome you into our family."

He huffs. "Well, they won't want me anywhere near them now."

"Funny how you've been so careful to avoid complicated relationships, and now you're involved in the most complicated situation I know."

He glances at me. "I deeply appreciate you believing

me."

"Of course, buddy. Why wouldn't I? It's not like you would keep something from me." I reply, hinting at the fact he *has* kept something from me.

"No, of course I wouldn't."

"Well, I'm sure my parents will come around— eventually."

Thane's eyes soften at the mention of my parents. "They're good people, Anderson. I enjoyed spending time with them." Then he adds with a smirk, "Although, I could have done without the whole cleaning of the stalls part."

Tears come to my eyes as I try not to laugh.

Hold it together. He's right where I want him.

"I have to say, your acceptance of my family brings tears to my eyes." Unable to contain it even a second longer, I explode in a burst of laughter.

"What's so funny?" he demands.

"I'm just seeing you in my mind—butt-naked, mucking out stalls."

"You were, too," he says in his defense.

I lean forward and whisper, "But you got pranked, buddy."

"What do you mean?"

I smile, confessing, "The naked stunt was all Pop's idea."

Thane's face turns a deep shade of red. "So, you're telling me your family doesn't really clean the barn in the nude?"

I snort and start laughing again. "Of course not! That would be impractical and completely unsanitary."

"That's exactly what I thought," Thane grumbles under his breath.

"But, bless your heart, there you were, strutting your stuff with Pop and me."

He pinches the bridge of his nose, shaking his head slowly. "I can't believe your father pranked me."

"Consider it an honor. He only pranks those he considers worthy."

"I was nude for nothing..." he laments as he crosses the room and plops down on his bed.

"Oh, it wasn't for nothing. Pop and I will be laughing about it for a long, long time."

Thane groans and covers his face with his hands.

"But I do have one question for you, buddy."

He looks through his fingers, giving me an exasperated look. "What?"

"What exactly do I say in my sleep?"

He sits up and looks at me strangely. "What has that got to do with anything?"

I raise an eyebrow in answer and watch with growing elation as the wheels start to turn in his head.

"Megan," he whispers.

"What about her?" I ask innocently.

"She not really in love with me, is she?"

"Why would you think that?"

He shakes his head in disbelief. "This was all an elaborate scheme because I never told you what you cry out at night."

I just stare at him, my grin growing bigger.

He starts chuckling with relief. "So, you really orchestrated all this?"

When I jump off the bed and take a bow, he breaks out in genuine laughter. "And I never suspected a thing…"

"I did warn you I'd get even."

"And you did," he laughs. "I've been sweating bullets, worrying about your sister, wondering how I was going to let her down easy when I hadn't done a damn thing."

"By the way, Megan did say you have a nice butt."

He blushes, his embarrassment amusing to see.

"So, now that I've revealed my hand, it's time to reveal yours. Do the right thing and tell me what I say at night."

"Are you certain you want to know?"

I spread my arms out wide. "You question that after all I've done?"

Thane smirks. "Fine. It's nothing shocking, just a little odd."

When he says nothing more, I prod him. "Well?"

"You cry out the word 'page' in your sleep."

"Ah…" I sit down slowly, my heart suddenly aching. "I wasn't expecting that."

DP with Glee

Now that I'm back in LA, glee and I have made it our goal to meet at the dungeon at least once a week. Between my college schedule and her new work hours, it's been hard to carve out the time together, but we're both determined to make it work.

Knowing that glee has an interest in new experiences, I approach Thane with a proposition I hope he'll agree to. Although he and I have done a threesome together once before, what I want will push the boundaries for both of us.

"Hey, buddy, I have a request."

Thane looks up from his textbook. "Shoot."

"I'd like to give glee a special scene, one she hasn't done before, but I'll need your help."

"Go on."

"I know she's enjoyed a myriad of scenes with the many Doms at the dungeon, but there's one she hasn't experienced yet. And, of all the men I know, you're the only one I would ask."

He closes his book. "Okay, now you have my attention."

"So…you remember that threesome we had on the beach with Rhythm?"

His lips curl into a smile. "Of course, I do. I have fond memories of that day."

"Well, I want to do something similar."

"What do you mean by 'similar'?"

I chuckle uncomfortably, uncertain how he will react to what I'm proposing. "I'd like glee to experience double penetration."

Thane says nothing, but it's easy to read the expression on his face. He's already envisioning what that will involve.

"Hmm…"

"Look, I know it may be a little awkward if our man parts rub together, but there's no way to prevent that with double penetration."

"I suppose not, when you're both fucking the same area less than an inch apart."

"Exactly. So, buddy, is it something you'd consider?"

"Is it something glee wants?"

"She's mentioned it several times but knows the Doms in our dungeon would never consider it."

Thane chuckles. "Yes, I could see it being an issue for most of them—an affront to their Dominance and manhood."

"Knowing that, are you willing?"

Thane remains silent for several moments while he considers my request. "I would, but not in the dungeon setting. I feel it would be better for the three of us if we take the audience out of the equation. I see no benefit to setting ourselves up for judgment or ridicule."

"Agreed."

"And, as this will be the first time for all of us, the less distraction, the better."

"I'm with you one hundred percent. I'll get us a hotel where we can have all the privacy we need."

"Good."

"Hey, I really appreciate this."

He nods. "I also have a vested interest in making glee happy. I owe her for the help she's given me in training Samantha, and I'm a man who likes to pay his debts."

"Good to know, because I want her first time to be everything she imagined—and more."

Chuckling, Thane says, "It seems I'm about to get to know you on a whole new level, Anderson."

I smack him on the back. "Kind of weird to think about it."

"More than a little odd, if I'm honest."

"If you feel that way, why did you agree?"

"I'm curious what it's like. How can I have an opinion one way or the other unless I try it?"

"True." I'm grateful that the guy has an adventurous spirit.

"So, when will you tell glee the big news?"

"Right now, actually. I'm going to surprise her at work and whisper it in her ear. I bet that will make the rest of her shift uncomfortably wet."

"Huh…Durov might be right," Thane says with a smirk. "You do seem to have a sadist streak."

I chuckle all the way down the stairs. There isn't

much I wouldn't do for glee, but this…this has got to be the biggest thing yet.

The fact that Thane has agreed to do it is a miracle.

I pick a hotel with good ratings, but still within my means. Someday, I plan to be rich enough where I don't have to worry about money but, for now, this boy has to be frugal and smart.

There's a sexual thrill trying something new and, in this case, it will be a new experience for all three of us. It puts this encounter on an entirely different level, and I'm buzzing with anticipation.

After borrowing a friend's car for the evening, I pick Thane up. On the drive to glee's place, I ask, "How are you feeling about things tonight?"

"Exhilarated," he says simply.

I glance at him and grin. "Me, too."

"I've been researching the ins and outs of double penetration, so to speak," he jokes. "It's recommended that you use plenty of lubrication, so I've brought extra to help glee accommodate your considerable girth."

"Good. I'm curious to see if glee will be able to handle it. I imagine it's one thing to fantasize about DP, and quite another to actually go through with it."

"Will she be allowed to use her safeword in case things get too intense?"

"Of course. The entire reason we're doing it is to please her."

"I'm glad we're agreed on that. Should things not as planned, we'll change tactics and find other ways to pleasure her tonight."

I grin. "Did you learn anything else during your extensive research?"

"Besides an abundance of lube, it's important you and I get the angles and rhythm right. I'm certain it will be a case of trial and error."

"Definitely glad we're not doing it at the dungeon," I snort.

"As am I. Glee should be our only concern."

"Absolutely, buddy."

"Is it safe to assume you'll be taking her vagina while I claim her ass?"

"Yes. Although glee enjoys the challenge of anal penetration with my cock, it makes sense for you to be the one to do it."

"It aligns with what I read. They recommend the man with the smaller of the two penises take that position."

I nudge him. "Don't feel slighted, buddy. I can't help being the bigger man."

Thane rolls his eyes. "Very funny."

When we pull up to glee's place, I suddenly feel nervous and sigh. "Here's hoping we do right by her tonight."

"I have every confidence we will."

Thane insists he stay in the car while I get glee.

"It's not necessary," I assure him.

"I disagree. This is your gift to her. I am simply here to help."

I give him a nod, impressed by his thoughtful consideration. In every way, Thane has proven to be a good friend.

I walk up to the door and ring the bell. One of glee's girlfriends from the dungeon answers and immediately lowers her gaze, but I can see the smile playing on her lips as she invites me in. "Glee apologizes, but she needs another minute."

Before I can even reply, glee comes bounding into the room and I'm left speechless. For the occasion, she's chosen to wear a flouncy white dress, and she has a flower in her hair. The perfect vision of a virgin.

"Well hello, beautiful."

Her eyes sparkle with excitement. "Should I call you Master or Brad tonight?"

"Master will do."

I hear the girl beside me gasp softly. I suspect glee has informed her about tonight's activities.

I hold out my arm to her and tip my hat to her girlfriend as I lead glee out the door. I'm surprised to see Thane has moved to the backseat of the car. Once again, it reminds me of how selfless he is.

Opening the door for glee, I help her inside and give Thane a nod of thanks.

"Good evening, glee," he says from the backseat.

She turns to face him, gushing, "Sir, I'm just so honored—"

"The honor is mine. I look forward to experiencing

this with you."

I see glee visibly shiver as she turns back around, and she buckles the seatbelt.

"Excited?" I ask her as I drive off.

"I haven't been able to think about anything else since you came to work and told me. That was so *naughty* of you, Master."

I grin in satisfaction, pleased to hear my plan worked.

Once we arrive at the hotel, Thane suggests the two of us register at the front desk. "I'll meet you at the elevator, so it won't be obvious we're together."

I appreciate that Thane is always looking for ways to protect those around him, but I tell him, "I'm sure that's unnecessary."

"Still, I insist."

"So be it." I take a small bag from the truck before taking glee's hand and escorting her into the hotel. After signing in, the two of us head toward the elevator.

Thane walks up just as the doors open and the three of us step into the elevator together.

On the way up, glee giggles nervously, looking at me than at Thane.

"Having second thoughts, glee?" I ask.

"No, Master. I just can't believe I'm such a lucky girl."

When the doors open, I place my hand on the small of her back and walk her to the room while Thane goes to unlock the door.

"Ladies first," he tells her, gesturing inside.

Once the door closes and Thane has it locked, I feel the sexual tension radiating like electricity between the three of us.

"How would you like me, Master?" glee asks.

I smile, telling her, "Naked and kneeling beside the bed."

A cute little squeak escapes her lips in response to my command. The ever-obedient sub, she takes the flower out of her hair and places it on the end table before she slowly begins to undress before us.

Her small, pert breasts beg for my attention, but I notice her shaved pussy is already swollen and wet. The girl must have been fantasizing about tonight the entire day.

I suspect if I were to barely touch her clit, I would make her come. But I want her to anticipate this moment a little longer as I stand there, admiring her.

Glee stands naked before us, wearing only my bracelet.

It's sexy to watch her kneel gracefully, her head down and her arms open in an inviting position.

I reach into the bag I brought and pull out a bottle of whiskey.

"Would you like some, glee?"

She looks up momentarily. "No thank you, Master." Returning to her pose, she waits as I take out two tumblers and pour Thane and myself a glass.

Handing it to him, I say, "Here's to a night we won't forget."

Thane takes the glass and raises it. "And to glee's many orgasms."

"Hear, hear," I agree, clinking his glass.

Glee wiggles her ass in her kneeling position, obviously appreciating our toast.

Thane and I drink the whiskey slowly, looking at each other as the two of us mentally prepare for the kinky scene ahead.

Personally, I'm praying I don't lose it the moment I sink my cock into her. I have a suspicion it's going to feel intense—incredibly intense.

Staring at Thane, with his calm but confident demeanor, I reflect on how fortunate I am that he's agreed to this. I know no other Dom I would be willing to open myself up to this intimately, especially with glee.

He's a full-on Dominant but, like me, he has a sensitive side—one that allows for encounters like this.

After we both finish our whiskey, I spontaneously decide to strip, and Thane follows suit.

Wanting to add to glee's experience, I command her to watch.

Her eyes grow wider, as her attention moves back and forth between us while she watches her two Masters baring themselves. It's easy to tell Thane and I are just as excited by the prospect of this union as she is, based on the rigidness of our cocks.

"How would you like to begin?" Thane asks me.

"I think kissing her is in order."

"Stand, glee," I command, holding my hand out to her. Glee takes it and I pull her to me, starting with a tender kiss that quickly grows more passionate as I slide my tongue into her mouth. The soft moan that escapes her lips makes my cock ache with desire.

Thane reaches over and caresses her small breasts while I continue to kiss her. Needing to feel how wet she is, I reach between her legs. The girl has never been this wet before, and a low groan erupts from my throat.

I'm ravenous and want to take her now, but I understand the importance of foreplay in a situation like this. It's essential we prepare her body for the rigorous challenge two cocks will demand.

I move glee to the bed and tell Thane to kiss her as I settle down between her legs. I spread open her swollen outer lips to expose her clit, taking a moment to admire its beauty before my lips descend upon it.

Glee lets out a muffled cry while kissing Thane, as I lick and suck her luscious cunt. I can tell she's dangerously close to coming by how much she's squirming. Rather than indulge in a little orgasm denial, I command, "Come for me."

She cries out, immediately tensing before coming against my tongue.

I stay still, relishing the feel of her pussy pulsating against my mouth. "Good girl…"

After the last pulse, I murmur, "Would you like another?"

"Yes, Master," she begs.

I smile as I go down on her again. I've always enjoyed the power of making a woman come with my tongue.

After her second climax, Thane leaves the bed to get something out of the breast pocket of his suit which is hanging over a chair. He shows glee a black length of cloth. "We're not going to gag you because we want to hear your sounds of pleasure, and we're not going to bind you because you need to be free to move, but I want you to be assured of your submission."

Thane places the thin cloth around her neck and ties it, stepping back to admire her.

Glee reaches up to touch the cloth around her throat and says with tears in her eyes, "Thank you, Sir."

The man is a genius. Glee hasn't worn a collar since the day her Master left the dungeon. By using a simple strip of cloth, he has claimed her as ours for the evening. And, based on the tears in her eyes, this is exactly what she needed.

"Are you ready, glee?" I ask huskily.

She looks up at me, her eyes luminous with desire. "Yes, Master."

While Thane coats his cock with lubricant, I coat my own hand before spreading glee's legs. I gently penetrate her ass with my fingers, coating the inside with a generous amount of lubricant.

She moans in pleasure, enjoying the sensitivity she experiences with anal play.

I then coat my cock with a thick layer of the lube, forcing myself not to think about what we are about to do so that I don't come too quickly.

I clean my hands, then head over to the bed and lay down. "Mount yourself on my cock."

She hesitates a moment, then bows her head. "May I ask something, Master?"

I sit up, concerned. "Of course, glee."

"If it pleases you, I'd prefer to mount Sir Davis and have you take me anally."

I glance over at Thane, wondering if it's wise to alter the plan.

Thane asks her, "Are you sure you can handle it?"

"I'm not sure, but I want to try, Sir."

Thane looks at me and nods. "She does have her safeword."

I get up from the bed, and Thane takes my place. Glee looks at him lustfully as she crawls across the bed and straddles his hips.

Grasping his cock, Thane guides her down his hard shaft, closing his eyes and groaning as she slowly takes the entire length of it.

I lay on the bed beside them, reaching up to caress her breasts while he begins thrusting into her. Glee throws her head back, moaning with pleasure as she grinds her pussy against him.

Unable to resist kissing her while she's being fucked, I change positions, kneeling beside her.

Fisting a handful of her hair, I pull her head back to claim her lips. There's something oddly erotic about kissing glee while she's being fucked—as if I am connecting with both of them.

When she reaches for my cock, I immediately command her to stop, knowing the extra stimulation will ruin any chance I have of maintaining control over my libido.

Like glee, I've been envisioning this all day and have no more patience, so I break our kiss and position myself behind her.

"Lay on him," I order her.

Glee lowers herself onto his chest, giving me full access to her cute little ass. I spread her cheeks apart and press the large head of my cock against her pink rosette.

"Ready, darlin'?"

She responds with a soft moan, answering with a breathy, "Yes."

I press against her tight opening, but it doesn't seem as if it's going to give even when I push harder against it.

"Bear down," I command.

As soon as glee does, I watch as my shaft begins to disappear into her ass. She moans loudly as she takes the full head of my cock. "That's it," I encourage her, guiding myself farther into her.

Her ass is incredibly tight with Thane inside her. The feeling is so incredibly intense, I'm forced to pause for a moment.

After the rush of an impending orgasm slowly abates, I continue to push my cock into her, groaning as I watch her take more of me.

Thane says in a low, seductive voice, "I can't tell you how sexy it is to watch Anderson take you while I'm inside you." When he begins kissing her, I feel her body relax, allowing me to push deeper.

I slowly begin stroking her ass with my cock, but the constriction is so unbearably pleasurable, I must stop again.

I wasn't prepared for it to be this intense.

I partially pull out, then push back into her.

"Oh, yes…" glee cries out as her body takes my shaft even deeper.

Spurred on by her passion, I start stroking her harder, pushing my cock in a little deeper with each stroke.

Glee not only enjoys it but cries out for more.

Thane has remained still the entire time, so I ask, "Are you ready to try coordinating our thrusts?"

"Are you prepared, glee?" he asks her.

"Yes! I want to feel you both moving inside me," she purrs.

Thane grasps her waist and begins to move slowly. The first time I try to move with him, I slip out, my cock slapping his balls on the way out.

I chuckle, repositioning my cock. "Sorry about that."

"Bound to happen."

Once he resumes his movement, I play with glee's nipples to loosen her body's resistance before trying again. After several successful thrusts, it happens again.

I'm feeling a bit mortified, but I'm not a man to give up easily. Changing my angle, I find better control and am able to match Thane's measured thrusts. Together, we find a rhythm that works.

The tightness and thrusting of another penis invokes a unique and immensely pleasurable sensation—not only for me, but for glee, as well.

"Harder, faster…please, Master."

"Harder and faster, you say?"

"Yes, *please*!"

I grasp her buttocks to control the depth of my thrusts and look down at Thane—both of us ready to rock glee's world.

I let him start, then begin thrusting with opposing stokes, matching his pace halfway. Glee's moans drive our movement as we begin increasing the rhythm of our thrusts.

Her sounds of passion grow louder and louder until she suddenly screams, "Yes, yes, yes…oh, my God, yes!

I feel the pulses of her orgasm as she comes around

my cock. With every ounce of resolve I have; I keep my own orgasm at bay.

After her climax ends, she whimpers, "Again…I beg you."

I look at Thane and confess, "I don't know how long I can last."

"I say we join her next climax."

Nuzzling her ear, I whisper, "Would you like that, glee?"

"Nothing would please me more, Master."

The two of us start again, slowly building the rhythm of our coordinated thrusts. I give in to the crowded, intense feeling that claiming her like this creates.

Thane cries out, "Fuck!" as he thrusts even faster.

I match his new pace, stroke for stroke, listening to glee's unintelligible cries of passion as she orgasms around my cock again.

With no reason to hold back, I grip her buttocks and let my impending orgasm tip over the edge as I release my seed deep in her ass.

For a moment, I lose touch with reality because my climax is so intense. After the last thrust, however, I suddenly feel as weak as a babe and pull out, collapsing beside them. "Holy hell, that was amazing!"

Glee looks at me, her whole body glistening with sweat. She's too weak to say a word, but her smile conveys everything she feels.

I reach up to caress her cheek. "Kiss me."

Leaning forward, she presses her lips against mine.

I gaze at her in admiration. "You are a mind-blowingly hot sub, darlin'."

She presses her cheek against my hand and murmurs in a hoarse whisper, "Thank you for tonight…"

She then turns to Thane, lavishing her kisses on him.

I lay back and watch, thoroughly satisfied, body and soul.

Embracing Loss

I've really buckled down with my studies the second part of the school year, not only to prove to my parents that I'm serious, but to also show Dean Abernathy and the entire staff that I belong here.

It's as if the library has become my new home.

Ironically, it seems that Thane and I have traded places. I'm now the studious one, and he's always looking to escape to the dungeon.

"What's got you so stressed out?" I ask him when he suggests heading back the very next evening.

"I don't know. I've got a bad feeling that has been haunting me for weeks."

"Do you think it has something to do with the Beast?"

"She's still in jail, and now that the press has been dealt with, she has no power over me."

A random thought hits me. "Do you think it's possible she's been a threat for so long, you don't know how to move forward without that stress?"

He looks at me for a moment, then nods. "It's possible."

"It may take a while, but you'll get used to it." Giving him a nudge, I add, "That or you'll end up spending your entire life at the dungeon."

He chuckles. "That wouldn't be so bad, would it?"

"It would, if you're still planning to get that house on the beach."

Thane snorts. "Actually, all I need to do is find a way to make a living at it."

I burst out laughing. "Yeah, that's bound to happen." I put my arm around his shoulders. "Let me give you some advice you once gave me, 'Get your head in the game, it's the only way to win at life.'"

He huffs. "It's not like I'm losing, Anderson."

"No, you're not. You just don't seem like yourself these days."

He lets out a ragged sigh. "Yeah, something's off and I don't know what it is."

"Take my advice—embrace your new freedom and do something productive with it."

Thane rolls his eyes. "You're sounding far too much like me."

Giving him a wink, I say, "I learn from the best."

Thane lies down on his bed with a far-off look in his eyes, then suddenly sits up as if he's just remembered something, and turns to me.

"You talked in your sleep again last night."

I suddenly feel disconcerted, an icy shiver running down my spine.

Fuck my subconscious!

"Since you've just given me sound advice, let me return the favor. What haunts your dreams at night?"

"I don't want to go there, buddy."

"We've done a threesome together. I think you can trust me," he replies with a grin.

I stare him down from across the room. "That may be true. However, it doesn't make me obligated to tell you anything."

Thane raises an eyebrow. "Are you going to make me do it?"

I frown, wondering what kind of game he's playing. "Do what?"

"Cash in on the debt you owe me."

My pulse starts racing, and I warn him in no uncertain terms, "Don't."

"This isn't a case where you get to choose."

Feeling trapped, I snarl, "If you're my friend, you won't."

"That's the thing. I *am* your friend, which is why I insist."

"You're calling it in now?" I growl, trying to suppress my rising anger. "There are a ton of creative and far more entertaining ways you can use it."

"Yes, but regardless, I am calling it in."

I stand up, clenching my hand into a fist. I'm beyond pissed! I do *no*t appreciate being forced to open up about something so personal, and all I want to do right now is punch the guy in the face.

But, unfortunately, I'm a man of my word and have no other choice but to honor my debt to him.

"So, you want to know why I cry out the word 'page'

at night?"

"I do."

"It's the name of a girl I knew."

He furrows his brow. "Someone you left behind?"

"In a manner of speaking," I say through gritted teeth.

"Explain."

I close my eyes for a moment and take a couple of deep breaths, trying to curb the desire to punch him and run. "Paige was my best friend. She was just a kid when she died."

Thane nods, processing what I've said before stating, "Life can be cruel and exceedingly unfair."

Tears come to my eyes and I barely choke out, "Yeah…"

His gaze is compassionate as he waits for me to continue.

I see Paige's smiling face in my head and have to swallow hard to force down the growing lump in my throat. "I was still a kid and couldn't accept her death…"

I go on to explain to Thane about being mute for months before I took up bull riding and the whip.

"So, losing Paige spurred on that risk-taking side of your personality?" Thane asks.

Hearing her name spoken aloud still causes a deep ache in my heart, and I turn away, suppressing all those unwanted emotions from rising to the surface. Clearing my throat, I answer, "I suppose you could say that."

"Anderson, I understand the impact loss can have on a person, especially when you're young."

Goosebumps rise on my skin. Until now, I hadn't

realized he would understand. Although our experiences are vastly different, the pain and confusion of losing someone at a young age still remains the same.

I meet his gaze, but my sight begins to blur as tears fill my eyes. "I thought I'd finally dealt with it. I even met with her parents and had a good cry over it this summer. But, apparently, I'm still a mess if I still call out her name and…"

"And, what?" Thane gently prompts.

"I'm afraid to commit."

"With glee?"

I nod, feeling embarrassed even as I admit it to him. "I don't want to open myself up to that kind of pain again."

"No one's forcing you to. Even though your parents mean well, they would never want you to go against your gut."

"But, that's just it. I *want* to take the next step with glee—but it's like, I can't. It feels as if I'm paralyzed inside."

Thane walks over and lays his hand on my shoulder. "I've learned from years of experience that loss is not something you get over. Grief is a long process, not a one-time occurrence. You've denied your grief for so long that you're just now moving through the full process despite how long ago it was."

"I hate this! I just want this feeling to go away," I tell him angrily.

He gives me a look of compassion. "It's the only way to move forward."

I shake my head, as stubborn to the core as I've always been.

"When you think of Paige, what's the first thing you feel?"

"An immense, black hole of loss…" The tears threaten to fall when I share that truth.

"Come," Thane says, wrapping an arm around me, "we'll mourn our losses together."

I see raw pain in his eyes and am surprised when tears start falling down his cheeks. Seeing his grief unleashes the floodgates of my own battered emotions.

If I thought I'd cried a lot in front of Paige's parents, it's nothing compared to the grief I release now. It seems unending, and so incredibly painful that I want it to stop.

Thankfully, Thane acts as my anchor, holding me in place while I suffer through the torture mourning brings. My sweet, funny friend who was ripped away from this world at far too young an age and who died alone, crying out for her mama…

I can't let that go. I will *never* be all right with it.

"She shouldn't have died alone," I tell Thane. "I should have come for her sooner, but I was so intent on buying that damn ice cream. Because of that, I wasn't there when she needed me most."

A fresh round of grief ravages through me as I swim in guilt.

But Thane doesn't let me drown in it. Instead, he tells me, "You did not fail her. You *must* let that go. Guilt will only slow the process of healing. Wallowing in it serves no purpose. Do you understand me?" He grabs my shoulders and shakes me, saying again, "You. Did. Not. Fail. Her."

I close my eyes, unable to accept it.

"Say it," he demands.

When I don't respond, he shakes me again. "You need to say it out loud."

I take a deep breath and let it out slowly, before meeting his gaze. "I can't."

Thane wipes the tears from his eyes. "If you are guilty, then how much more am I? I knew my mother was having affairs and said nothing. By keeping silent…" His voice falters. "…I killed my own father. The man I loved most in the world."

"That's insane. You're totally innocent."

His gaze falls back on me. "What about you?"

I lie down on my bed and stare up at the ceiling, utterly exhausted on an emotional level I've never felt before.

But I also feel calm despite the storm of emotions I've just endured. "I didn't fail her," I state with more conviction than I feel.

"Good. Keep saying that to yourself whenever the guilt starts to overwhelm you."

I glance at Thane. His eyes are red rimmed from crying, and I suspect I must look equally as bad. "How's that working for you?"

"Some days better than others," he admits. Thane lies down on the bed beside me. "But, I'm definitely better than I was."

I hold my hand out, and he grasps it.

"Thanks for wasting that debt I owed you on me."

"I can't think of a better way to use it."

"I owe you one," I blurt, immediately regretting it as

soon as the words escape my mouth.

Thane chuckles but says nothing.

Thane has no idea that he has inspired a fundamental shift in my way of thinking. Knowing that the grief I feel over Paige's death isn't going to end, I resign myself to enduring it instead of running from it.

That pivotal change seems to break down the barriers surrounding my heart, but I'm not aware of it until I meet Dominus Leo.

He's come to visit the dungeon, having been invited by the Dungeon Master himself. There are underlying grumblings within the group about having an outsider allowed temporary access after the division the dungeon has just suffered.

However, it turns out that Dominus Leo is experienced in many aspects of BDSM. His gregarious nature makes him a welcomed addition to our more conservative group of Dominants.

Not only is Dominus Leo knowledgeable as a Master but, being a world traveler, he has a wealth of entertaining stories about places I've never been.

The man fascinates me, and I stand by proudly to watch when he asks glee to scene with him. Knowing glee's love of new experiences, this is a once in a lifetime opportunity I would never want her to pass up.

He gives her the choice of candle wax, needle play, or the violet wand for the scene.

"They all sound wonderful, Dominus," she answers graciously.

He smiles but reminds her, "You must choose one."

Glee doesn't hesitate. "I'd really like to experience the violet wand."

"Very well."

He glances at me. "Have you ever used one?"

"No. I didn't even know they existed."

"You'll find this interesting, then."

Dominus Leo leads glee to a binding table and tells her to strip. Once naked, he helps her onto it and secures her in the bonds. I notice glee tense up when he places a hood over her head.

I've noticed other Doms using hoods before and can only imagine the helpless feeling it must invoke, especially when bound to a table the way glee is. It's a vulnerable position for any sub, but it's made even more so when scening with a new Master.

However, I'm relieved when Dominus Leo asks her, "Color, glee?"

"Green," comes her muffled answer.

Dominus Leo's reassuring touches seem to relax her as he explains, "I am going to set the electric wand on medium and adjust it from there."

She nods from under the hood.

I see her jump when he turns it on, and the sound of the electrical charge fills the dungeon.

Dominus chuckles pleasantly. "It's a noisy thing, but I'm sure you'll agree that's part of its charm."

He runs the instrument up her leg, and she giggles. "It tickles, Dominus."

"Oh, so you'd like it stronger?"

He adjusts it, and the instrument buzzes louder.

Dominus Leo surprises her by touching her inner thigh, and she lets out an excited yelp.

"Color?"

"Green."

I can tell by the change in glee's voice that she likes the stimulation of the instrument. I immediately decide to save up for one so I can surprise her on her birthday.

Dominus Leo keeps amping up the power, and glee continues to respond exceedingly well to it, crying out in pleasure as he grazes her nipples with the instrument.

I actually enjoy watching him play with her. Dominus understands a woman's body, and he knows exactly how to stimulate glee with the electric wand. The combination makes for a successful scene everyone can enjoy, including observers like myself.

Once he's finished, he moves over to her and reaches between her legs to confirm her arousal. She squirms under his touch, clearly wanting him to take her.

That when I feel it—that first twinge of jealousy. I haven't encountered it before and wonder at its cause. I've watched numerous men take glee and have only felt inspired by glee's pleasure.

Tonight, however, something's changed. I turn and walk away, confused by the unfamiliar emotion.

Later that night, as I lie in bed, I feel I'm finally ready to walk to the edge and explore what a deeper connection with glee looks like.

And I understand exactly what I need to do.

The Wild Ones

I contact a local leathersmith that our Dungeon Master told me about and head over to his shop after class. It turns out the man works out of his garage.

He leads me to a worktable and shows me his current collection of collars for sale. "I recommend one with a ring. I make them strong enough so that you can use them during play."

I pick up a black collar and pull on the silver ring to gauge its strength. I'm impressed by his work. Setting it down, I pick up one that is thinner, a little more feminine, and dyed a dark purple. I play with the buckle in the back and imagine securing it around glee's throat.

"This is the one," I announce, handing it to him.

"Wonderful. Let me box that up for you."

I walk away feeling a mixture of nervousness and excitement as I clutch the box in my hand. This is a huge commitment. Every time I question whether I'm ready or not, all I have to do is think of glee.

I'd be a fool not to commit.

Pop's right. I'm not the kind of guy to play around for the rest of my life. I want to have a good woman by my side, and glee meets my needs both in and out of the bedroom.

If I were to see any other Dom's collar around her neck, there's no way I'd forgive myself. However, I keep silent about my plans to collar her.

Not even Thane knows.

I've been a risk-taker all my life—except when it comes to relationships. I'm sick of being a coward in that department and am ready to take that leap with glee. I can't let the fear of loss have that kind of power over my future any longer.

I'm a grown man. It's time I start acting like one.

Thane and I meet Durov at the dungeon that night. I can tell just by looking at the Russian that he's stressed out. Since that's unusual for the guy, I ask him what's going on.

"This semester has been an absolute bear," he complains. "I have so many tedious research papers and projects due that I don't have time for anything else. It's not right to waste time with such pointless things. I can't wait until this year is over!"

He lets out an angry growl and glares at me as if it's my fault.

"Hey, look. I hear ya, man," I chuckle with sympathy. "Between school and glee, I don't seem to have a moment to myself."

"Is that a problem?" he asks, suddenly interested in my affairs.

I glance at Thane, who is standing beside me, and grin at them both. "Actually, no. In fact, I like it so much I'm going to do something about it."

I hear glee's muffled cry nearby and excuse myself from the conversation so I can watch the scene she's participating in.

I'm not entirely surprised to see that she's with Dominus Leo again, although I would have preferred it if it was someone else. This time, the experienced Dom is using wax on her.

My cock hardens as I watch him pour drops of hot wax on the sensitive lips of her pussy. He has her gagged, but unbound, so she is free to squirm and wiggle.

Dominus Leo commands glee to remain still as he drips the hot wax over her pussy again. This time, she doesn't move, although she lets out another muffled cry.

Watching glee's willing submission to his wax play is a total turn-on for me. I enjoy their scene, but my gaze keeps going back to glee's throat, imagining how she's going to look with my collar around it.

When he begins removing the wax from her skin with a knife, I interrupt him. "Dominus Leo, I would like to speak with glee after you're finished."

He looks up, surprised by the intrusion, but then smiles when he sees it's me. "Certainly, Master Anderson."

I notice when Dominus Leo looks back down at

glee, there's a flicker of something more than friendship in his eyes.

I finger the loose collar in my pocket possessively.

Once he indicates he's done, I command glee to dress and take my hand.

She looks at me tenderly as she grasps it.

"I have something important I need to talk to you about," I tell her as I take her to a private room in the back.

"Wonderful! I have some exciting news to tell you, as well." Her eyes sparkle with a joyous light that makes me smile.

I lift her hand to my lips and kiss it before I escort her into the small room.

"Can I go first?" she begs after I close the door.

"Of course. Ladies first," I say gallantly.

"You know how crazy my schedule has gotten?"

I nod, expecting her to tell me she's quitting.

"I don't even have time to breathe anymore."

"Yes, I'm *very* aware of that."

"Well…" She bites her bottom lip for a moment, before blurting out, "I've been given the opportunity of a lifetime."

I cock my head, interested to hear what it is. "What kind of opportunity, glee?"

"You know how I told you I would love to travel?"

A knot starts forming in my stomach, but I answer calmly, "Yes."

"Well, Dominus Leo is offering to take me with him to travel around the world."

"Really?" I start fingering the collar in my pocket

nervously.

Glee smiles at me. "You know I care about you, but this opportunity is something I've always dreamed of."

"I know it is," I tell her, knowing how important it is to her based on our past conversations.

"The best part?" she says with a squeak. "He has friends around the globe—experienced Doms like himself who have all kinds of kinky talents."

"You do love new experiences…" I agree, realizing all is lost.

"So, I was thinking of saying yes to his offer." She looks at me earnestly, "I hope you understand."

I let go of the collar, taking my hand out of my pocket to caress her cheek. "Your happiness means the world to me. You should know that."

She stands on tiptoes to give me a kiss. "I'm so grateful to hear you say that. I was hoping you'd feel that way." She giggles, clapping her hands together in excitement. "I get to quit my crappy job, travel around the world, and experience all kinds of new kink. I can't believe I'm so lucky!"

I always knew she was a free spirit, I remind myself.

I sweep my hair back and force a smile. "I couldn't be happier for you, darlin'."

"So, what's your big news?"

I chuckle awkwardly, feeling extremely uncomfortable now. But, as I look down at glee's sweet face, I know what I need to do for both our sakes. "This couldn't have happened at a better time, really. I actually brought you in here to let you know that, as much as we enjoy each other's company, I don't feel like things are progressing between us."

"Oh," she says, sounding surprised.

"So, you can imagine my relief to hear your happy news. It's almost like this was meant to be. No hard feelings."

She grins, her eyes sparkling again. "Agreed. No hard feelings. We started as friends and we're ending as friends."

Even though I feel sick to my stomach, I look at her tenderly. "But, no matter what, these arms will always be open to you, darlin'."

She melts into my embrace and purrs, "Thank you, Master."

Realizing she will never call me by that title again once she leaves, I tilt her chin up with my finger and say, "That's Brad to you."

I'm silent on the way home, lost in a mix of conflicting emotions.

When Thane and I get back to the dorm room, he gives me a nudge. "What's up, Anderson? You've seemed out of it all night."

I figure there's no reason to keep it a secret from him, so I take the collar out of my pocket and throw it to him.

Thane stares at it for a moment before realizing the significance of it. "You were going to ask glee tonight," he states, rather than asks.

I snort. "Yeah, perfect timing, huh?"

"You still can go through with it. I'm sure glee would choose to wear your collar and stay if she knew your intentions."

I shake my head and sit down on the bed. "Yeah, but it wouldn't be what's best for her."

Thane walks over, sitting beside me. "How are you feeling?"

"Shell-shocked, mostly." I sigh, still not believing how everything went down tonight. "Thank God I didn't make that leap."

"What? Asking her?"

"No. Letting myself fall in love. I was close—been teetering on the edge for weeks now."

"So, you're not brokenhearted?"

"No, but I'm damn sad." I turn my head away. "I'm going to miss that girl…"

"We all will," Thane says despondently. "The dungeon won't be the same without her."

"No, it won't." The idea of her not being at the dungeon anymore sends a chill through me.

"Is that it, then?" Thane asks. "Are you done with love now?"

I glance over at him and chuckle. "No, I'm not a cynic like you. I still believe in love. I've been thinking about it and realize I need to be more thoughtful in my choices."

"What was wrong with glee?"

"She's so experienced and hungry for more, I doubt I could have been enough for her in the long run. I need to set my sights on the wild ones."

"Wild ones?"

"Yeah, the girls who don't know about their submissive side yet."

"You mean vanilla girls?" he asks, sounding surprised.

"Yeah, if I introduce them to the lifestyle, we can progress together without worrying about competing with our pasts. When I fall in love, it'll just be me and the sub I've trained, with a lifetime ahead to explore our kink together."

"Sounds to me like you already have someone in mind."

"Nah, but I'll know it when I find her," I tell him confidently.

Thane pats me on the back. "More power to you, my friend. As for me, I'm going to stick to the sidelines. It's much safer there."

But I whole-heartedly disagree.

"Never give up on of love, buddy."

Steamy Sendoff

There we are, the four of us gathered in the commons area outside, sitting in the grass, enjoying the warm California sun together. Samantha's lying against Durov, who has his arm around her, while Thane leans against a tree and I lay, spread-eagled, on the ground.

I turn my head toward Samantha. "So, I never asked. How did it go with your parents over the break?"

I hear her low growl of frustration.

"That well, huh?"

She purses her lips. "Rytsar already knows this, but I don't mind sharing with you. My parents were not understanding, in the least. My father told me that they've already suffered the loss of one child, but because of my deviant lifestyle, they feel they've lost two. Neither of my parents wanted anything to do with me after I told them."

I prop myself up with my forearms. "That's terrible."

"How could they be that short-sighted?" Thane snarls. "You're their only daughter."

"Not anymore—according to my father." Samantha retorts.

I see anger flash in Thane's eyes. "It's not right!"

"Do not fret, comrade." Durov says calmly, smiling seductively at Samantha. "She can stay at the beach house over the summer, if she wants."

"But my mother caused this," Thane growls. "Because of her, you felt pressured—"

"No," Samantha corrects him. "Telling my parents was purely *my* decision. I don't regret it. If my parents can't accept me for who I am, then I'm better off without them. Fuck it."

I can see she's hurt, despite her bravado. "You're not alone, Samantha. Think of us as your family now."

Thane agrees. "You can always count on me. I won't leave your side, no matter what."

Durov gives her a wicked grin. "If we are family, then you and I are committing incest, sister dear." He lets out a low growl.

She laughs as she grabs the back of his neck and they kiss.

"Enough you two," I blurt good-humoredly.

I'm hesitant to voice my idea, but it's been rolling around in my mind ever since glee said that she was leaving. I have no ill feelings toward the girl.

I still care about her, like all my past girlfriends—and I always will.

However, I'm not the only one who is going to miss glee. She's played a significant role in all our lives, so I decide to throw caution to the wind.

"You guys know glee's leaving at the end of the

week…" I toss out there.

Durov grunts in disapproval. "I have decided to hate Dominus Leo. He is stealing away all of our fun."

Samantha looks over at me. "I agree. I'm not happy with the man at all."

Thane sighs heavily, glancing at her. "I can't imagine our lessons continuing without her."

Samantha nods, looking disappointed.

"I know it's easy to blame Dominus for this, but glee's a free spirit. She was always meant to leave us," I confess, knowing it's true. "Traveling's in the girl's blood. He just happened to be the first person to offer her the world."

"I'm surprised you're okay with this," Durov states, sounding upset.

I shrug, telling him, "You can't keep what you never had."

"Well, I for one am *not* okay with it," he growls. "She was my favorite sub in the dungeon. What am I supposed to do now?"

Samantha gives him a seductive kiss. "You could always let a certain Domme teach you how to kneel."

Durov laughs. "The day I kneel to another is the day vodka rains from the sky."

She smirks, telling him, "Maybe that can be arranged."

Durov pinches her butt and she lets out an unconvincing reprimand.

We all know she enjoys it.

"I had a thought…" I continue.

Samantha starts kissing Durov, ignoring the rest of

us. Those two are still hot for each other after all this time. Seriously, it's so intense, I'm beginning to think it's unhealthy.

"Go on," Thane encourages me while they kiss.

"What if all four of us give glee one last scene?"

Samantha breaks their embrace and turns to me. "All four of us at one time?"

"Yes," I answer, drawing the word out as I look at the three of them.

Thane leans forward. "A proper sendoff."

When Durov doesn't say a word, we all stare at him, waiting.

He looks at each of us gravely before announcing, "It's perfect."

"Good! Then we're all agreed."

Remembering Thane's advice concerning the privacy of our threesome, I ask them, "Where do you think we should do it?"

"In the dungeon," Durov insists. "She gave up her Master when the group split so she could remain with us. There is no other place it should be."

I glance at Thane. "What do you think?"

He mulls it over for a moment. "In this case, I believe Durov is right. It won't simply be a sendoff from us, but from everyone at the dungeon."

Thane turns to Samantha. "Any objections?"

She frowns. "I think you're forgetting that I've never been invited to join the dungeon."

"If Dominus Leo can invade our dungeon, then the dungeon Master should have no problem allowing her one-time access for this occasion. After all, he created this situation by inviting the man," Durov states with a huff.

"I will personally plead Samantha's case to him," he adds, biting her on the lip.

We lose the two for several minutes while they have a biting match.

Thane rolls his eyes, but I see the smirk on his lips. We both find their pairing odd, but also incredibly entertaining.

"Since those two are preoccupied, we get first pick on positions," I announce to Thane. "I'm claiming her ass again for the scene."

"Then I claim her mouth," Thane states. "Glee is quite talented with that tongue, and I want to experience it one last time."

Durov's answer is muffled as he continues kissing Samantha. "I claim her pussy."

Samantha pulls away from him, looking annoyed. "And what does that leave for me?"

"Everything else," he growls huskily.

"I have no problem taking turns with her mouth," Thane tells Samantha. "In fact, I think glee would prefer it."

She smiles at him. "I like that idea."

"Then it's settled," I declare. "Durov will get permission for Samantha to join us at the dungeon and we'll send glee off one extremely happy sub."

Even though finals are looming, the four of us take the night off to give glee a proper goodbye. Although she has no clue about our plans, the rest of the dungeon has been informed, and a special area has been set up for the scene.

When we enter with Samantha in tow, I hear the whispers start up as the Doms around us openly admire the striking Domme.

Glee cries out in joy when she spots the four of us, but she's clearly surprised to see Samantha. "How is this possible?" she gushes, keeping her gaze to the floor as we approach. "All of my favorite people here on my last night?"

"We've come to say goodbye," I inform her. "And, to give you something."

"I'm so honored?" she says, bowing deeply before us. "Now I'm dying to know what you got for me."

"It's not what we got for you, but what we're going to give to you," I explain, dragging out her anticipation.

She giggles to herself. "Okay, then. What are you going to give me?"

"A scene," Durov tells her.

She glances up and smiles. "Lovely!"

Looking at Samantha, obviously thinking the scene must be with her, she asks, "What will we be doing, Mistress?"

Samantha's bright red lips curl into a smile. "It's not just me."

Glee looks at all of us, her gaze finally landing on me. "You, Master Anderson?"

I nod.

"And me," Durov states.

Her eyes grow wide as she looks at Thane. "And you, Sir?"

"Yes, glee."

She puts her hands to her mouth and starts jumping up and down in excitement. "Oh, my goodness! All four of you at the same time?"

We nod in unison.

She looks around at her friends. "Can you believe this?"

"Lucky girl…" one of the other subs says, jealousy tainting her voice.

"Do you consent?" I ask.

"Are you kidding me? Of course, Master." Tears come to her eyes as she looks at us. "I'm deeply honored by this gift."

Glee kneels before us, her gaze on the floor, and says with awe in her voice, "Thank you."

"Stand and serve your Masters," I command.

With grace, she rises from the floor. I walk her to the central area reserved for us. The only furniture for the scene is a bed set on a raised platform so everyone will be able to watch, and a side table with instruments.

Samantha walks over to glee and begins undressing her. The three of us stand back, admiring the beauty of the exchange. As Samantha unclothes her, she leaves kisses on different parts of the girl's body. Soon, glee is peppered with the red impressions of the Domme's sensual lips.

Once glee is free of her clothes, Thane commands her to kiss each of us. She turns to Samantha first, and I stand there, my cock growing unbearably hard as I watch these two women kiss each other passionately.

Glee then moves to Thane, who fists her hair, kissing her deeply as he presses his body against hers. She responds to him, melting into his embrace.

Rytsar is next. Grabbing her by the throat, the Russian is rough as he claims her mouth, and her moans of pleasure fill the room.

Glee then moves on to me. "Master…" she whispers as our lips touch. Knowing this is our last time, I kiss her the way I know she likes to be kissed, starting out slow with a tender kiss that grows more ardent as my tongue enters her mouth. We get lost in our kiss, and I don't realize I've taken too long until I hear Durov clear his throat.

I give her a wink as I break away and release her from my embrace.

She stands before us, seemingly a little dazed while she waits for her next command.

"Undress your Masters," Durov orders.

Glee smiles, turning to me first. I relish the feel of her touch as she unbuttons my shirt, slipping it off my shoulders. She then kneels, helping me out of my boots and socks. Looking up at me with sultry eyes, she stands again. Biting her bottom lip, she slowly unbuttons and unzips my jeans. My cock stands at attention as she pulls my briefs down along with my pants.

Glee carefully folds my clothes into a neat pile, then faces me, smiling as she runs her hand over the bolo tie around my neck before turning to undress Durov.

She treats each Dominant as if they are the only one

in the room, making it sensual to watch while she undresses each one.

When she is finished, Samantha commands, "Stand before us so you can take pleasure in the bodies of the four Dominants who will be challenging you tonight."

Glee stands with her hands at her sides, palms up in an inviting pose, as she looks at each of us, her eyes luminous with lust.

Knowing that I am the first, I take the lubricant off the table and tell glee to coat my cock with it. I grit my teeth to keep my desire under control as her expert hands rub the lube evenly over the length of it.

I lie down and command her to stand next to the bed. Reaching between her legs, I play with her swollen sex.

Damn, the girl's hot down there…

I lick the taste of her from my fingers before telling her to mount me reverse cowboy style.

She squeaks in excitement as she crawls onto the bed.

I hold my shaft in position and take one of her hands to help her balance as she slowly takes my cock into her ass. I don't hold back my groans as I watch her grind herself on it until she's taken the length of it.

"Good, girl," I growl lustfully.

Reaching around her, I grab her breasts in my hands and tell her to lie back against me. I release a breast to cup her chin and turn her head. Then I kiss her while tugging at her nipples, my cock wedged in her tight ass the entire time.

If this isn't heaven, I don't know what is.

Now that glee's breasts and pussy are exposed, the others can partake of her.

Samantha climbs onto the bed first, a set of nipple clamps with a chain in her hand. I feel glee tense as the Domme attaches the first clamp to her left nipple.

Glee's breathing increases as she watches Samantha pinch her other nipple and attach the second clamp. The girl whimpers softly when Samantha starts tugging on the chain.

Samantha leans down to kiss her, pulling the chain harder as her tongue enters glee's mouth. I have the best seat in the house while I watch the two tongue-wrestle each other.

Durov enters the picture next, playing with glee's clit as he coats his own shaft. Samantha stops what she's doing and lays back to watch while Thane lies down on the opposite side of me. He cups glee's breast, teasing the clamped nipple with his tongue.

When Glee squirms in pleasure, it gives me pleasure, as well. I have to close my eyes, trying to ready myself mentally for the intense stimulation.

In this position, I have far less control and will have to rely on the Russian to control the rhythm of our thrusts.

Durov cleans his hands, tosses the towel on the floor, and moves into position between glee's legs.

Samantha and Thane stare at glee's face, wanting to see her expression when Durov pushes his cock into her.

I, however, close my eyes to concentrate on the pleasurable tightness of glee's body as Durov's shaft slowly sinks into her pussy.

Being an experienced sadist, he knows what he is

doing and makes no missteps as he starts ramping up his thrusts. I grab glee's waist with both hands, partly for leverage and partly so I can try and match Durov's pace.

Glee screams out, "I love it. Oh, God, I love it!"

Thane changes position, kneeling on the bed beside glee so his cock is level with her mouth, and commands her to suck him. She immediately grabs his hard shaft and opens her mouth, bouncing with each thrust of Durov's cock as she sucks.

All of this is an overload of stimulation. So much so, I force myself to think of other things to keep from coming too fast as Durov and I coordinate our movements and start thrusting faster.

I glance over to see Samantha playing with herself as she watches Durov fuck glee. With one hand she yanks on the chain attached to glee's breasts, making glee moan loudly as the clamps pull at her sensitive nipples

It seems to be exactly the stimulation glee needs, because she suddenly starts shaking uncontrollably as an intense orgasm flows through her and around me.

"Faster, Durov," Samantha cries, fingering herself more vigorously.

Glee's moans get louder the faster Durov pounds into her.

I'm on the fucking edge as I watch Samantha's pussy start pulsing as she comes right beside me.

It's like a chain reaction: first Samantha, followed by Thane, who comes in glee's mouth, and then, finally, Durov and I stiffen as we ready to climax.

Glee pulls away from Thane cock and screams out in pain and pleasure as the two of us come inside her at the same time.

I can't move afterward, paralyzed by the intensity of my own orgasm. I watch as Samantha straddles glee's face, which is just above mine, and commands, "Eat my cunt and taste my come."

Samantha's blonde pussy is red, wet, and swollen.

I swear if I could have, I would have come again when Thane reaches over and begins playing with glee's clit while she eats Samantha.

The moment Samantha climaxes, glee immediately joins her, and Durov and I are both pushed out as glee's body contracts in pleasure around our spent shafts.

I chuckle to myself afterward, my mind blown.

This wasn't a gift to glee; this was a gift to all five of us.

Hours later, when it's finally time to leave the dungeon, glee takes me aside.

"I want to thank you again. I was told you were the one who orchestrated tonight's surprise."

"It was my pleasure, glee. Truly."

"It's something I'll never forget. Ever." She looks down at the bracelet on her wrist and undoes the fastening.

"Don't you want it?" I ask her, surprised when she hands it to me.

She blushes. "I do, but I thought you'd want it back."

"Why? I had it made for you."

"Good," she says, putting it back on before reaching

out to touch the stone on my bolo tie. "Because I want you to keep this for the very same reason."

"Are you sure you want to leave your lucky stone behind?"

Glee giggles softly. "Yes. I'm already the luckiest girl in the world."

I gaze down at her tenderly. "I agree. Dominus Leo seems like a good man."

She wraps her hands around my arm. "You're a good man, too."

I glance around the dungeon, feeling wistful. "You're going to be missed, glee. And, not just by me."

"I'll definitely miss everyone here."

I shake my head, grinning at her. "You've got a whole world to explore. You won't have time to miss anything—and that's exactly the way it should be."

"You are a remarkable man," she says, squeezing my arm. "I can't wait until we meet again someday, so you can tell me about all the incredible things you've accomplished."

"I look forward to that day, as well," I tell her, hopeful it will happen. "I suspect you'll have some *fascinating* stories to tell."

I give her a chaste kiss on the cheek before walking her over to Dominus Leo.

Holding out my hand, I give the man a firm handshake. "Safe travels."

"Thank you, Master Anderson."

I smile and nod to them both before turning to leave, feeling no regret as I walk away.

Glee is exactly where she's meant to be.

Unexpected Complications

The week of finals, Thane comes barging into our room, shouting, "I can't fucking believe this!"

I need to study for my Applied Calculus test, but I can see he's incensed. So, I put down my pencil and close the book. "What's up?"

When Thane meets my gaze, I can tell immediately that he's spooked.

"Seriously, buddy, what's wrong?"

"Thompson just called. My mother received her sentence today. After having her mental state evaluated, the courts found her mental health condition requires treatment."

"Isn't that a good thing?"

"No. The damn judge sentenced her to time served, adding ten months in a mental institution. In ten months, she'll be free." Thane starts pacing. "They're transporting her to a facility this week." He looks up and yells at the heavens, "I just want to be free of that woman!"

I grip his arm, looking him straight in the eye. "We've got your back. You know that. And we have plenty of time to come up with a plan to protect you from her."

"I don't want to do this anymore, Anderson. I'm done." The look of defeat on his face guts me.

"Don't let her get in your head. This is finals week. You're close to crossing the finish line! Remember when you told me you planned to graduate a year early? I didn't believe you then, but you are right on track. Just one more year." I slap him on the back, trying to cheer him up. "You're almost there. Can't you taste it?"

The only response I get is a forced smile.

"So, sit your butt down at your desk and forget everything else," I say, guiding him to his chair.

He sits but continues to stare at me looking dejected. In a monotone voice, he says, "What does it even matter?"

"It matters because you are a man of your word. You promised yourself you would do it, and you need to honor that promise."

Thane chuckles sadly.

"Do right by yourself. Don't you dare think of giving up now."

Thane's expression changes, and I hear him growl under his breath. "Yeah, I can just imagine her laughter if she hears I failed this semester and quit."

I like seeing his fighting spirit reappear. "That's right, buddy. No way are you giving the Beast that kind of satisfaction."

"No, I won't."

Encouraged by his change of attitude, I take a textbook from his backpack and place it on his desk. "So, do what you need to do and stick it to your bitch of a mother."

I watch with satisfaction as he slips on his earphones, gets his notes out, and opens a textbook.

No man left behind…

I've decided that's my new motto as I sit down at my own desk and dive back into my studies.

Five days later, I am ready to celebrate! I've fucking slayed all my tests and feel like a conqueror.

I invite my friends to a kegger party I've heard about being held off campus, but only Samantha agrees to join me.

Durov claims he's already committed to hanging with his Russian friends for a night of vodka. He tells me after the semester he's experienced, he *needs* to drink them all under the table.

As for Thane, he's been lost in his own world ever since he got the news about his mother. The guy successfully made it through finals this week and is still on track, but it seems as if the wind has been taken out of his sails.

So, Samantha and I go by ourselves to enjoy some end-of-the-year partying, and we stay until the cops arrive to kick everyone out. Walking back to the campus, I find I'm pleasantly buzzed.

"I never knew you were such a party girl, Samantha. You're really fun when you let your guard down."

"I have many different sides to me," she says with a playful grin. "I'm as complicated as they get."

She stops for a moment, balancing on each foot as she takes off her heels, carrying them in one hand as she continues walking with me.

"Those things must hurt like a motherfucker. I don't know how you do it."

She shrugs. "I like the power they give me, so I actually don't mind the pain." She holds one of the shoes up threateningly, the spike pointed right at me. "Plus, they make great weapons if anyone tries to get fresh."

I raise my hands in surrender, chuckling. "You don't have to worry about me."

"I know." She smiles. "But I still figured I'd warn you."

"I didn't realize you could be so feisty."

She laughs. "I've been told I get that way when I'm tipsy. You should see me when I drink tequila."

"I'm suddenly craving Mexican food. What do you say?"

She gives me a sideways glance. "I see what you're doing there, but I'm not drinking margaritas tonight."

I chuckle. "You just have me curious, is all—"

Samantha suddenly stops and points. "Is that Rytsar?"

I look in the direction she's pointing but see nothing. "Where?"

"On the ground," she cries as she starts running toward him.

I follow her and see Rytsar sprawled out on the ground next to his dorm, a smile planted on his face.

"Looks like someone did a little too much celebrating," I comment as I grab his hand and help him to his feet.

Samantha drops her shoes to help support him. "We'd better get him to bed."

We walk him into the building which seems unusually quiet for a Friday night. "Guess everyone's still out partying."

"Yeah," she laughs. "We're the only responsible ones here."

As we wait for the elevator, Durov turns his head toward Samantha. "Well, hello, beautiful."

"Hey, my drunken Russian."

When the doors open, Samantha tells me, "I can take it from here."

"You sure?"

"Absolutely," she says, winking as the doors close.

I leave the building, laughing to myself. I've never seen Durov that drunk before but, based on the smile on his face, I assume he's found his happy place.

I'm surprised I don't see Thane when I arrive back at our dorm. I trust everything is okay, but I wish he'd joined me tonight so I wouldn't be worrying about him now.

When it gets to be two in the morning, I head outside to search for him. After wandering around fruitlessly for a half hour, I head back in, realizing it's pointless. I have no clue where he might be.

I start pacing the room to calm my rising anxiety,

wondering if his mother has gotten out somehow. Who knows what the damn woman is capable of?

Finally, after three, I hear Thane fiddling with the doorknob. When the door opens, my stomach sinks. The guy looks as pale as a ghost.

I walk toward him, my blood running cold the moment our eyes meet, and I see the look of horror on his face.

"What the hell happened to you?"

"Not me. It's Durov…"

I hope you enjoyed *Master's Fate!*

Coming next—*The Russian Reborn: Rise of the Dominants Book Three*, the final book of the trilogy

The story of these young Doms continues in this explosive ending!

Find out what happens to Rytsar, Sir, Master Anderson, and Samantha. The fallout is going to blow your mind.

IT'S EXPLOSIVE!

Read the next book
(Release Date – June 25, 2019)

Or, if you are new to Brie and the gang, you can begin the journey with the 1st Box Set of
Brie's Submission which is FREE!

Read the 1st box set

COMING NEXT

The Russian Reborn:
Rise of the Dominants Book Three
Available for Preorder

Reviews mean the world to me!

I truly appreciate you taking the time to review
Master's Fate.

If you could leave a review on both Goodreads and the
site where you purchased this eBook from, I would be so
grateful. Sincerely, ~Red

Don't miss the stories of the Sir, Rytsar, Master
Anderson, and Samantha that you read about in
Master's Fate.

You can begin the journey with the 1st Box Set of *Brie's
Submission* which is FREE!

Start reading NOW!

ABOUT THE AUTHOR

Over Two Million readers have enjoyed Red's stories

Red Phoenix – USA Today Bestselling Author
Winner of 8 Readers' Choice Awards

Hey Everyone!

I'm Red Phoenix, an author who also happens to be a submissive in real life. I wrote the Brie's Submission series because I wanted people everywhere to know just how much fun BDSM can be.

There is a huge cast of characters who are part of Brie's journey. The further you read into the story the more you learn about each one. I hope you grow to love Brie and the gang as much as I do.

They've become like family.

When I'm not writing, you can find me online with readers.

I heart my fans! ~Red

To find out more visit my Website
redphoenixauthor.com
Follow Me on BookBub
bookbub.com/authors/red-phoenix
Newsletter: Sign up
redphoenixauthor.com/newsletter-signup
Facebook: AuthorRedPhoenix
Twitter: @redphoenix69
Instagram: RedPhoenixAuthor
I invite you to join my reader Group!
facebook.com/groups/539875076052037

SIGN UP FOR MY NEWSLETTER
HERE FOR THE LATEST RED
PHOENIX UPDATES

SALES, GIVEAWAYS, NEW
RELEASES, PREORDER LINKS, AND
MORE!

SIGN UP HERE

REDPHOENIXAUTHOR.COM/NEWSLETTER-
SIGNUP

Red Phoenix is the author of:

Brie's Submission Series:
Teach Me #1
Love Me #2
Catch Me #3
Try Me #4
Protect Me #5
Hold Me #6
Surprise Me #7
Trust Me #8
Claim Me #9
Enchant Me #10
A Cowboy's Heart #11
Breathe with Me #12
Her Russian Knight #13
Under His Protection #14
Her Russian Returns #15
In Sir's Arms #16
Bound by Love #17
Tied by Hope #18

*You can also purchase the AUDIO BOOK **Versions**

Also part of the Submissive Training Center world:

Captain's Duet
Safe Haven #1
Destined to Dominate #2

Rise of the Dominates Trilogy
Sir's Rise #1
Master's Fate #2
The Russian Reborn #3

Other Books by Red Phoenix

Blissfully Undone

* Available in eBook and paperback

(Snowy Fun—Two people find themselves snowbound in a cabin where hidden love can flourish, taking one couple on a sensual journey into ménage à trois)

His Scottish Pet: Dom of the Ages

* Available in eBook and paperback

Audio Book: *His Scottish Pet: Dom of the Ages*

(Scottish Dom—A sexy Dom escapes to Scotland in the late 1400s. He encounters a waif who has the potential to free him from his tragic curse)

The Erotic Love Story of Amy and Troy

* Available in eBook and paperback

(Sexual Adventures—True love reigns, but fate continually throws Troy and Amy into the arms of others)

eBooks

Varick: The Reckoning

(Savory Vampire—A dark, sexy vampire story. The hero navigates the dangerous world he has been thrust into with lusty passion and a pure heart)

Keeper of the Wolf Clan (Keeper of Wolves, #1)

(Sexual Secrets—A virginal werewolf must act as the clan's mysterious Keeper)

The Keeper Finds Her Mate (Keeper of Wolves, #2)

(Second Chances—A young she-wolf must choose between old ties or new beginnings)

The Keeper Unites the Alphas (Keeper of Wolves, #3)

(Serious Consequences—The young she-wolf is captured by the rival clan)

Boxed Set: Keeper of Wolves Series (Books 1-3)

(Surprising Secrets—A secret so shocking it will rock Layla's world. The young she-wolf is put in a position of being able to save her werewolf clan or becoming the reason for its destruction)

Socrates Inspires Cherry to Blossom

(Satisfying Surrender—A mature and curvaceous woman becomes fascinated by an online Dom who has much to teach her)

By the Light of the Scottish Moon

(Saving Love—Two lost souls, the Moon, a werewolf, and a death wish…)

In 9 Days

(Sweet Romance—A young girl falls in love with the new student, nicknamed "the Freak")

9 Days and Counting

(Sacrificial Love—The sequel to *In 9 Days* delves into the emotional reunion of two longtime lovers)

And Then He Saved Me

(Saving Tenderness—When a young girl tries to kill herself, a man of great character intervenes with a love that heals)

Play With Me at Noon

(Seeking Fulfillment—A desperate wife lives out her fantasies by taking five different men in five days)

Connect with Red on Substance B

Substance B is a platform for independent authors to directly connect with their readers. Please visit Red's Substance B page where you can:

- Sign up for Red's newsletter
- Send a message to Red
- See all platforms where Red's books are sold

Visit Substance B today to learn more about your favorite independent authors.

Manufactured by Amazon.ca
Bolton, ON

14736871R00140